My Father The Mafia Boss

GIGLIOLA CASTANIA' LEGGIO

Published by Gigliola Castania' Leggio

Publishing partner: Paragon Publishing, Rothersthorpe

ISBN 978-1-78792-028-6

Book design, layout and production management by Into Print

www.intoprint.net
+44 (0)1604 832149

Some of the royalties from this book will be gifted to the people of Corleone, although my father Luciano Leggio, was a cruel heinous man. The people of the town welcomed me in 1986 with friendship and love. This is my way of saying thank you.

Gigliola Castania' Leggio

Dedicated to Antonio, a kind, wonderful man. Who brought Salvatore and I together. Our Sicilian matchmaker. May your spirit always be with us.
Gigliola.

One

SHE SAT AT the side of her mother's bed, the doctor had been blunt after this last heart attack. There was no second chance; her mother would die. It was only a matter of time. She tried to feel some remorse but the two had never really got on. Her mother seemed to blame her for some past wrong. She had never known what it could have been, always trying to be a caring daughter. Yet her brother Graham had always been the favourite. Even when he went off the rails and ended up in prison, he was forgiven without question! Oh, but if she dared forget to phone at the required time, she got it in the neck for days. How could a mother love one child so deeply while having such contempt for the other?

Realising that she did not have much time left, her mother decided it was time for her daughter to know about the heavy weight that she had carried on her shoulders for many years. Why she despised her daughter as she did. It took 10 minutes to unburden her soul. As a Catholic, should she not have done this to a priest in confession? Was this the last despicable thing she wanted to do to her daughter?

Graham was just coming up the corridor when Janice rushed past, knocking him as she went. He called after her but then, on the sudden realisation that maybe their mother had died, he ran into the room. He was relieved to see his mother smiling at him as best she could.

"What was wrong with Janice?" he asked, confused.

His mother never answered, gesturing with her hand that he should sit beside her. Janice meanwhile fled to her car, and accelerated from the car-park, just missing a car as it was coming in. She just drove until she found herself at her 'be alone' spot. The reservoir, where she could find peace and quiet from the madness of everyday life. It was all too much to take in; was this just another act of cruelty to her by her mother? Or was the life she had known until now been a complete lie? What did she do with this new-found knowledge, bury it forever? Her mother would soon be gone. She did not want to hurt her mother and she had tried so hard to be loved by her. But nothing she had ever done had been right in her mother's eyes. Even when she married Charlie, her mother couldn't see how good he was for her. Was it right that the child should be blamed all her life so far for her mother's failings? Was it her fault that the Catholic Church banned abortion? Did her mother really hate her with such a passion? Then why hadn't she had her adopted? Sent her to someone who would have loved and cherished her? Was everything due to Catholic doctrine, was this her mother's way of paying penance for her previous wrongdoings?

With so many questions swirling around her head, she had been sitting there for hours. It was getting dark and now she had to come back to reality, but she didn't know what that was anymore. Charlie her husband would be able to offer some words of advice. Oh God, Charlie; it just got worse. How would he feel to discover the woman he had married might not be the person he thought she was? She began to get angry; she wanted answers from her mother, and she wanted them now! She had to call at the garage for some fuel; the reservoir was some distance from the hospital. It was then that she realised that at this time they might not let her onto the ward, so it was better for her to go home. As she opened the front door she was greeted by a furious Charlie.

"Where the hell have you been? Graham rang hours ago, said you had stormed out of the hospital. Did you have a problem with your mother again? She's sick for God's sake."

She said nothing but just went into the kitchen and put the kettle on.

"Well Janice, what the hell is going on?"

"Oh, please don't. I just need some space. My mother told me something. I can't explain now, it's all spinning around in my head. I'm trying to make sense of this on my own. If I don't understand, how can I explain it to you?"

Charlie flung his arms around her and held her tightly; she didn't want him to let her go. In this moment she was safe, in the reality until a few hours ago she had always known. She knew deep down that she would have to tell him at some point what her mother had told her. But this could wait until she was sure he needed to know. He withdrew from the embrace, made some strong tea and ushered her into the front room. He topped her tea with a nip of brandy and sat her down, covering her with the throw, as he could see her shaking physically. She sipped tea sitting quietly, her mind racing behind her façade. Then suddenly she began to speak.

"Charlie, I don't believe my mother. What have I ever done to her? Have I not cared for her every time she's been sick? Where was Graham? Too busy in his world to care. I tell you Charlie, I bet he gets every penny of her money."

"Is money what worries you? For God's sake, Janice, we're fine, we don't need your mother's money."

"Of course, it's not the money; he can have it all. The only thing my mother ever did for me was to give birth to me; she even resented that. It's just the injustice of all this. Because she had to be mean to me all these years. Well, now I have some idea," she said before she realised. Angry at herself as her husband raised his eyebrows as if to signal, she had better explain.

"So, what does that mean?"

"I told you I don't want to talk about it now!" She got up and walked up to the stairs.

"I'm going to have a bath and then go to bed. It's almost midnight so I think I'm just going to go to bed; are you coming?"

"I'll be up in a minute." Charlie got himself a whisky and sat in his chair; what the hell was going on? 'Families' he thought to himself.

Little did he know as he finished his drink, the bomb that was about to explode. How would he react with this new knowledge? What would it mean to him and Janice?

He knew it had something to do with her mother? A long-held secret, which she decided needed to be unlocked before she died. He could see the profound effect on his wife, which was obvious to him. If only she would let him in. Then, if he continued to nag her, she might never tell him. He would stand by her until she was ready to tell him about it. He turned off the lights and went up to bed; tomorrow was a new day.

Charlie turned in bed to cuddle up to Janice, but she wasn't there; he pressed the button on the clock bedside table, which told him it was 5:30am. He slipped out of bed and threw on his bathrobe and went downstairs, Janice lay under the throw on the couch. A half-drunk cup of what looked like camomile tea was on the coffee table. He gently whispered her name, not wanting to startle her; eventually he had to give her a slight nudge and she opened her eyes.

"What are you doing here?" he asked as she turned and sat up.

"Oh, I couldn't sleep, so I thought a cup of tea could help, it looks like it did, I was going to go back to bed. I guess sleep just got the better of me."

"Hey, you don't have to be sorry. Coffee?" Charlie asked.

"No, just a little tea, oh and you can put some toast on. I'm so hungry; with everything that happened yesterday I forgot to eat anything."

"Tea and toast it is then." Charlie went to the kitchen leaving her alone with her thoughts. She was still confused and so angry, so angry that for years she had been forced to live a lie. Angry that her mother felt the need to unburden her soul now; why not on any of the previous occasions when she had been so ill? Was it now because she knew this was the last curtain call? Her thoughts were interrupted by Charlie with her tea and toast; he gave her a brief smile and sat down with a mug of coffee.

Graham sat at his mother's bedside. She had fought all night, holding his hand until she fell asleep. He knew from her breathing that time was running out. He found it difficult to accept. They had been here on two previous occasions, but she had always rallied; a pacemaker helped her steer an even course."

"Graham, are you there?" she struggled to say.

"Of course, I'm here." He reached out and took hold of her hand.

"I left a will in my desk in the dining-room."

"Oh, mum, it doesn't matter now, don't worry about this, you're not going anywhere yet." He knew, of course, that he was being diplomatic with the truth, more to console himself. She wasn't stupid and knew her hours were numbered.

Janice was sitting at the dressing table when Charlie entered the bedroom. She looked at him through the mirror.

"She's dead, isn't she?" Janice said without a sign of emotion in her voice.

"Yes, about 10 minutes ago, Graham was with her. So, she didn't die alone."

"Oh yes I bet he was. Good old Graham, the little lapdog until the end."

"For God's sake, give it a rest. You went on about

10

your mother always having a go at you. But you're no better; give the poor sod a break."

"What, a fucking break, you bastard." She yelled at Charlie and threw the hairbrush in his direction, skimming his left ear as it passed him and hitting the bedroom door.

"Well, that's childish; for God's sake show some respect. She was your mother after all."

"For God's sake! That's all you ever say, I'm going to have it carved on your headstone," she said, mocking him.

Charlie decided he wasn't in the mood for his wife's vitriol and went downstairs. He wanted to support her, but she kept secrets from him. Not only that, but he had always had a way to get on with her mother. Yes, she could be vindictive and always spoke her mind, but he admired her. It was right that whatever her faults were, she was now treated with respect.

Moments later he heard Janice come down.

"I'm going out!" she shouted as she slammed the front door.

Charlie wondered if she was going to the hospital to see her mother.

She wasn't going to the hospital, but to her mother's house. She had an idea; a couple of weeks earlier while channel hopping, she had ended up watching a programme about a house clearance company. They were clearing the house of an elderly lady who had recently died. Rather than doing it themselves, the family had hired this company to do it for them, to sort what was worth auctioning and what was destined for landfill.

As she watched, she noticed in this house on TV that

there was a Victorian desk, which looked like the one her mother had. This did not have one, but *two* secret drawers in which important documents were kept. This meant that anything of a private nature would not be seen by the staff. Maybe her mother's desk had the same drawers. She thought it would be better to go this morning before her brother decided to empty it. He would like to see it on the market as soon as possible. She had always been told that there would be nothing in the will for her! She had been a lousy daughter, a huge disappointment to her mother, so she deserved nothing except trash from the trash can. She frowned to herself when she thought of how Charlie could not see why she was not in tears with the death of her mother.

The house felt eerie, almost as if it knew its mistress would not be returning and it was itself in mourning. She went straight into the dining-room, putting the *Daily Mail* she had taken from the mat on the table. Then she went straight to the desk, and lowered the lid. She threw her head in her hands because she could not remember where the hidden drawers were on the desk, which she had seen on TV. Now she also realised that this desk bore only a slight resemblance to the one on TV. She pushed various pieces of wood that seemed unnecessary. She was ready to give up when she had a sudden moment of recall. There was some beautiful carving at the bottom of the pigeon holes, so she pushed it, waiting for the sound of a click to say it was open, but alas nothing happened. So, she tried to push her hands down below. Voila. It lifted and then, tilting it outwards, it came off the front of the desk to reveal a hidden space.

There was a large dark brown envelope that she could

see hidden inside; she pulled it out. It had an old-fashioned wax seal stuck on it and a label with the date March 1956. Then there was another smaller white envelope that was unsealed. So she opened it first. It contained a deed poll certificate that read that the person named Margherita Castania had changed her name to Nora Shawcross. So, was her mother Spanish or Italian? She decided to stop and make tea before opening the sealed bag.

Then realising that there would be no milk, she settled on a glass of water; she went back to the desk, sat in the chair and took the large brown envelope, sliding her finger along the edge to open it. She picked up various pieces of paper and what looked like tickets. There were three letters, all in what she was sure looked like Italian writing. Her hypothesis turned out to be correct, the tickets were one for a one-way ferry ride from Palermo to the Italian mainland, then a train ticket from Naples to Paris. It was the final document that left her with a sick feeling in her stomach, and it was proof that what her mother had said on her deathbed had been the truth. It was a birth certificate issued through the Italian Embassy in London. The baby was registered as Gigliola on February 22, 1956. The name of the mother was registered as Margherita Castania, the name of her father Luciano Leggio, employment recorded as farm manager. She was physically shaking and had to run to the kitchen to be sick in the sink. Who the hell was Luciano Leggio? She swilled her face with cold water, then went back to the desk and replaced everything in the envelope including the deed poll certificate. So, the journey to find out who her mother, her real father, and in-fact herself were, had now begun.

Two

WHEN SHE WENT home, she saw a note from Charlie that said he had gone to his office, he said Graham wanted to talk to her and that she didn't have to cook, he would bring a Chinese for tea. She slipped her shoes off and went to put on the kettle. Then went upstairs to swill her face. Tea made, she then went and sat down at the dining room table and pulled the brown envelope out of her bag spreading the various contents on the table. Action plan? That was it: just where did she start?

She used the old envelope as an improvised notepad. The first thing she needed to know was who her mother really was? Why did she leave Sicily, then end up in the UK, and why did she feel the need to change her name? Surely she would have an accent, so people would know she wasn't English?

She realised that until she knew what the letters said it was pointless to make notes, what could she write except a series of questions and no way for now to be able to answer them? She went to the drinks cabinet pouring a large whisky and then, the glass in one hand bottle in the other, went and sat on the couch. Reaching across to the sideboard she took hold of a picture frame; it held a photograph of the man she had always known as her father. She held him close to her and cried, tears flowing over her face.

When Charlie arrived home, Janice was slumped on the couch, the bottle of whisky almost empty, sleeping like a little girl. Charlie noticed papers, strewn across the dining table through the open door as he took the Chinese to the kitchen to keep warm in the oven. Then he went back to help his wife.

"Come on honey, we'll put you upstairs where you can sleep comfortably."

It took a good attempt to get her to her feet, then he lifted her into his arms and took her to the bedroom. He put her on her side in case she was sick and pushed a pillow into her back.

Once downstairs, he thought he might as well finish the last bit of whisky, poured it into a glass, took the empty bottle in the kitchen and took out his half of the Chinese. Sitting at the dining table he looked at the objects, it was the ferry ticket that caught his eye. Why would his wife have this, then he noticed the date? Relieved that she had no intention of leaving without telling him. He was more intrigued by the three letters and birth certificate, a little confused when he saw that it had Janice's date of birth on it, but not her name, and other names he did not recognise. He decided it was best to go check that Janice was ok, so he left the papers on the table and took his plate and put it in the sink and went up to bed.

She still lay exactly where he had left her; she seemed so quiet, he didn't want to disturb her, so he went to sleep in the spare room. He was not so lucky with his sleep, he tossed and turned, who was Margherita Castania. More importantly, who was Gigliola and what did she have to do with Janice? Maybe she'd give him answers in the morning?

Next morning it was Janice who woke up alone still with her clothes on top of the bed. She turned her legs around and put her hand to her head, boy she had a hellish hangover. She was on her way to the bathroom when Charlie appeared at the top of the stairs the glass in his hand.

"Bad head? This could help."

"I'm sorry I drank most of your single malt," she said, taking the glass.

"What's going on Janice?"

"Oh the papers you saw them. I am sorry I did not put them away."

"Look, take a shower, then come for breakfast if you think you can eat something. We can talk about it?"

Charlie turned and went back downstairs. Janice went to the bathroom swallowed the soluble aspirin and went in the shower. Well, then she had no choice but to tell Charlie. After her angry outburst yesterday and then getting drunk he had every right to know what it was all about.

He stood looking into the garden, Janice went up to him and cuddled in his back and then he turned and kissed her.

"Bacon and eggs?" he asked.

"No, just toast please and a very strong coffee."

Charlie knew that his wife had to feel groggy since she very rarely drank coffee, even then it was weak. In his eyes it was not worth drinking to that strength.

"So, what is it. Do you feel ready to tell me now?" He waved the letters and the certificate at her.

"The day before my mother died, she told me she wasn't English. Her parents and in fact she herself were Sicilian. That my father was not Archie, but a man named Luciano Leggio. She said it was up to me if I wanted to trace him, he was still alive. That if I tracked him down, I was not to judge her, she hoped I'd understand."

"That's why you ran away from the hospital and almost pushed Graham to the ground?"

"Yes."

"But how did you find the birth certificate, these letters?"

"Believe it or not quite by accident." Janice told him about the desk and the secret drawer.

"So, what are you going to do? Are you going to look for this man?"

"I think I should start with the letters, have them translated. Then contact the Italian embassy."

"I've already rung them; I hope you don't mind and as for the letters my friend Luigi at the pizzeria he will translate them into English for me."

"Oh, Charlie that's so sweet of you, you're sure you don't mind."

"No, I don't, hell if it was me, I'd like to know who my father really was."

Meanwhile at their mother's house, Graham had begun to sort through the mountain of clutter that was there. It was such a big house, and their mother had never thrown anything away. Empty bottles, newspapers. It wasn't until she had a stay in the hospital that they could thin things out, oh, but she always knew. But it was too late then, they had gone to be recycled. He was looking at some old photographs. When he noticed that in one Janice seemed crippled, she was trying to walk leaning forward, with what looked like two umbrella handles for walking sticks. He couldn't remember this at all. There were other photos showing them in fancy dress for Children's Day. Janice had won one year as a mermaid; the costume that was made by their mother. He gave an ironic smile, they had been happy moments when they were children; it was when their father died, that everything seemed to go wrong. Especially between mother and daughter, both strong willed and stubborn. He had always been shyer. Janice said he just sucked up to their mother. When he was ashamed to tell her, he was being controlled by her. Now, with her gone, he could rebuild his relationship with his sister. There was no doubt that he would share any inheritance with her, their mother was not here to block it.

Charlie had gone to work, and when he came home at teatime he had called in the pizzeria and Luigi had translated the letters in the best possible way. But he had struggled, one of the letters was in Sicilian dialect, and not your daily Italian, but he was able to translate enough to make them understand the gist of what had been written. He was eager to tell her what had been gleaned from the letters.

"Janice, are you in?" he called up the stairs.

"Yes, just changing the bed, be down in a minute."

She appeared in the kitchen with bedding in her hand and put it in the washing machine.

"Come and sit down, I have some information for you."

"Ok, just making some tea, you want coffee?"

"No thanks." Charlie opened his briefcase and took out the letters and their translations. Then read again what they said while waiting for Janice to join him.

"Right then are you ready?"

"As I ever will be."

"Ok, the first letter is from your mother's father to a man named Dino Cammarota. Your mother fell in with the wrong crowd and got pregnant. Her mother disowned her for bringing shame to the family, she wanted her expelled from home and sent away."

"Is that why she went to Naples?"

"Yes, her father wanted an advance on his salary so he could get her a ferry ticket to the mainland. He had a brother who lived in Naples. The second letter simply said that she could go and stay with them and work in their bakery to cover her food and lodging."

It was the third letter that dealt the killer blow. This was not pleasant to read. Her uncle was furious that he was not told that Margherita was pregnant; if he had known that he would not have agreed to take her in. Especially when she told him who the unborn child's father was: Luciano Leggio.

"Then why should it be important that it was this, Luciano?"

"The birth certificate tells its story."

"Don't they say they're not proof of identity on their own?" Janice suddenly decided she wasn't sure she wanted to accept all this.

"Yes, it is true, we will have to wait until we hear back from the Italian Embassy."

"Well, I'd better sort some tea," Janice said taking the letters from Charlie and putting them in the desk drawer.

"No, let's eat out, I fancy a good steak, what do you say?"

"Ok, give me ten minutes to change."

Both ate in silence, Janice was desperate to know who Luciano Leggio was, from the sound of her mother's uncle's letter he was not a really kind man to know. Luigi knew only too well who this man was. Charlie hadn't told his wife, he hoped she would decide not to go into the matter further. It would be better for everyone if she didn't.

A new day dawned, Charlie went to the office as usual, leaving Janice to paint in the conservatory she had turned into a makeshift studio. She heard the phone and went to answer it before the answer phone came into play.

"Hi Graham, how are things going. Are you at the house?"

"Yes, can you come round, I could do with a hand?"

"Of course, I'll clean my brushes and I should be there in about 30 minutes if that's ok?"

"Great, see you then."

When she arrived, Graham was trying to clear some of the items from the front bedroom; she tried to open the door to facilitate her entry, but there was so much piled up behind the door that it was hard to move it.

"Good God Graham, how much stuff can you get in a bedroom?"

"Yes, I think that's what the TV show calls hoarding."

"It's knowing where to start, there's a lot of furniture," Janice said as she tried to free her leg from the side of a large trunk that was in front of the dressing table, which for some reason was in the middle of the room.

"Well, if we move the chairs into the spare bedroom that will give us more room to move." He had snapped at Janice when she said he would simply be transferring things from one place to another, so he wouldn't really be achieving anything. She suggested they have a cup of tea, then she could tell him what she didn't feel able to do on the phone.

They decided to go and sit in the back garden; it was a pleasant afternoon, they could sit in the shade near the beech. Janice took a long sip of her tea, breathed in and then just blurted it out.

"Archie wasn't my real father." She waited for a reaction from her brother.

"What, don't be stupid of course he was. Why would you say that?"

She closed into him on the bench and took his hand.

"When I stormed out of the hospital, it was because mother had just told me."

He took his hand away. "No, you're lying, it's not true."

"I have the evidence."

"Evidence, what evidence?"

"Letters written by her family, our mother was not English, she came from Sicily."

"No, she would have told us. She would never betray us." Graham became agitated and, like a spoiled child who had a tantrum, threw his cup on the grass.

"You had better go, I won't listen to this trash."

Janice could see how upset he was and decided that

yes, it would be better to let him digest what she had said. She would tell him the rest when he asked her to.

When she got home, Charlie was relaxing on the couch watching the snooker on TV.

"Drink? You look as if you need it."

"Oh, Charlie he…" She began to cry. Charlie got up and gave her a hug.

"Look sit down I'll give him a call; he might listen to me."

Janice nodded her head and sat drying her tears from her cheeks. Once he got her a whisky, he went on the phone. She could hear Charlie talking to Graham, it would seem he wasn't in the mood yet to listen.

"He hung up, said I was a party, it was a kind of a conspiracy to cheat him with the money your mother left behind."

Graham stood with the decanter in his hand, fighting the temptation to have a drink. He'd been on the wagon since he was released from prison. Was he going to fall off the wagon now, would he let his sister's lies drive him to it? He rushed into the kitchen pouring the contents of the decanter into the sink, before throwing it against the wall; it smashed on impact sending shards of glass across the kitchen floor. He slipped down the cupboard door until he made contact with the tiles and sat there sobbing, he hadn't cried like that since his day in court. His defence of being in the wrong place at the wrong time, dismissed by the jury and found guilty.

The telephone rang, the answer phone clicked on. The sound of his mother's voice set him off again, the grief of his mother's death finally hitting home.

Three

JANICE WAS TRYING to paint, but her thoughts were captivated by poor Graham. It would be just as hard for him to accept all this, as it had been for her. But they had always been close ever since they were children. This didn't need to change anything between them. Her thoughts were interrupted by the phone, she thought it would be Charlie, so she was surprised it was her brother.

"You had better come to the house and bring your proof." He sounded very officious, but she was glad he had rung; it was a start. She cleaned her brushes, went and changed out of her painting smock, slipped on a flowery dress. She decided to walk to their mother's house, she felt the knot twisting in her stomach. When she arrived, she thought it best to ring the doorbell.

"So, did you bring the evidence?" Graham growled at her.

"Can I sit down first?"

"Oh yes sorry, I didn't mean to be so matter of fact."

They both went into the lounge and sat opposite each other, like patients in a doctor's waiting room. Janice opened the bag and pulled out the faded brown envelope, then getting up took it to Graham. He slowly removed the contents and sat down to read the letters before looking at the English versions. It was when he looked at the last letter, he seemed to start shaking physically, the blood drained from his face, he seemed to look as if he would faint at any moment.

"Graham" Janice said, "What's wrong?"

"Leggio," he just mumbled "No, it can't be true."

"You know him. Who is it?" Janice was anxious to know.

"Remember when I had my sabbatical, I went around Europe. I stayed in Milan for a week or more, it was all over the media."

"Leggio - why, is he a movie star, a writer?"

"You've never heard of him, you don't remember seeing him on the news, he was everywhere."

"Ok ok, I'm sorry I'm still none the wiser."

"I hope this is someone's idea of a sick joke. Luciano Leggio was the leader of the Sicilian Mafia; had been on the run for years. But he was tracked down in Milan and arrested."

It was Janice's turn to be light-headed.

"Oh my God, Graham this is like being stuck in *The Godfather*."

"Apparently Mario Puza based his book on a Sicilian Mafia Don."

"Is that all you can say, just throw in that little fact so casually?"

"Then, what do you want me to say? What does

Charlie think?"

"He was like me; no idea."

"No, he must have, we were..." Graham paused just in time. He quickly changed track and felt he had almost escaped.

Janice decided that she no longer wanted to talk about it and that she needed to start cleaning the desk and cupboard, so her mind would otherwise be occupied.

"Did you order a skip?" Graham shook his head, so she took the yellow pages and phoned a local company called Preston's, who could deliver skips at short notice.

"There is a small box in the desk with photographs inside, you might find it interesting, some are of us in fancy dress."

"Oh, do you remember when they did that drunk driving campaign on TV, Mum did you up as a drunk driver with your head all bandaged, your arm in a sling."

"With cold tea in a bottle, so it looked like whisky." Graham laughed.

"Happy times, do you know what's wrong with me here?" She took out the image of her struggling to walk.

"No, I've seen it, but I have no recollection of it; Maybe mother..."

"It's all right Graham, it takes some time to get used to the fact that she's no longer here, especially for you as you spent more time with her."

Graham looked at her, as if to say she shouldn't have said that, then said he would start to clear the bookcase. He had cleared two shelves, putting the books in boxes placed on the table with labels on the front, so each box had the relevant subject. He had just begun the third shelf when he gasped.

"Good God who would have expected to see this?" He took out the book and waved it at Janice.

"It's a book."

"Well observed, but it's about the Mafia."

Graham went and took it to his sister. She snatched the book from him and went straight to the index, sliding her finger down the Ls until she found his name.

"What are you looking for?"

"Yes, he's here, look at this."

"Yes, so what?"

"Pott's disease."

"I'm sorry."

"Perhaps that's what's wrong with me. I could have Pott's disease."

"So, I still don't understand what it has to do with reading something in a book about the Mafia?"

"Look, it says that Leggio had suffered from 'Pott's disease' since he was a child, had spinal problems and walked leaning forward like me in this photo. You don't see it could be a link? If it can be hereditary, it could reinforce the evidence that he was my father."

"Janice, do you want him to be?" Graham seemed disappointed by his sister, what of the man they grew up calling dad? Was she just going to forget Archie just like that, replace him with this atrocious man? Then if he were really her father, would it be so wrong. But wouldn't she want to disown him rather than embrace him?

"Can you remember much of his arrest?"

"Oh, let's not go there sis, let's wait and see what happens."

"But if you can tell me anything, what does he look like." She was almost pleading with him.

"Little fat guy, the cigar in mouth, your typical mobster. I think you'd better go; this is a lot for me to take in without facing an interrogation." Graham got up and took the book from her, threw it on the floor, then almost manhandled her to the front door.

"My bag!" she cried. He went to get it and slammed the door in her face.

Janice walked into the town centre and went to the bookstore. She went in and stopped when she saw the eager assistant waiting to help her.

"Good afternoon how can I help you?" She asked.

"Do you have any books about the Mafia, in Sicily in particular?" There, she had asked; the assistant would have no idea why she wanted them, so she should relax a little. She didn't have 'Daughter of a Mobster' tattooed on her forehead.

"Organised crime, that section is towards the back of the store, some people are a bit nervous around such books, so we like to have fashion, gardening in front of the house so to speak, if you want to follow me." The assistant took her to a large bookshelf near the fire exit.

"There are a number of books, I'll let you browse at your leisure." That said, she disappeared back to the counter.

There were a lot of books about American gangsters, she guessed they were mobsters of one kind. It wasn't something she'd really thought about until now. She took out two or three possible books, but there was no mention of Leggio. Had he yet to arrive in such books? She finally found what she was looking for. Carrying them as best she could to the assistant. Slowly placing them on the counter.

"So, are you interested in crime? So many books about the Mafia in particular, are you doing a degree?"

"Something like that, research into Sicilian/Italian crimes." She was a little annoyed by the young woman's insinuation. Then she scolded herself, this comment was just meant to engage in a polite conversation, nothing more. Books paid for, she entered the market square to use a pay phone. She didn't feel like taking the bus home; a taxi would be more advantageous; after all she had quite a few books to read. She was disappointed that there were no books just about Leggio; maybe he was not as important as Graham had made him sound when he had spoken briefly about the Mafioso's arrest. While she was waiting for the taxi she had a thought, she could go to the reference library the next day; they would surely have newspaper reports and she could learn about him that way.

Once home she paid for the taxi and walked up the driveway, there was no trace of Charlie's car, so he wasn't home yet. Great she thought, she could go get some tea and start her journey into the world of the Mafia. Time can pass in the blink of an eye, and so absorbed in the books, Janice had not thought about what she and Charlie would have for their evening meal, and before she knew it, he came in from work.

He was less than impressed when he saw all the books lying on the dining table and no pleasant aroma emitted from the kitchen. They argued, it was the first time Leggio had come between them. Charlie was worried that his wife was becoming a little too obsessive about the Mafia, highlighting his frustration by sweeping all the books on to the floor. He turned around and stormed out of the front door. Janice heard the gravel as he turned his car at speed and was gone.

Picking up the books she replaced them on the table and went to see what was in the fridge, she really should eat something. Not all that hungry she made a ham sandwich, boiled the kettle for some tea and went back to her books. It was fascinating but disturbing in equal measure. The evening passed, there was still no sign of Charlie, and her eyes were beginning to hurt. So, she took herself off for a nice relaxing bath in some bubbles. Then decided that she was sitting up no longer and took herself to bed.

When she woke up it was 6-30, she was alone in bed. Not too concerned she thought Charlie might have slept in the guest room, but he wasn't there; looking through the window she saw that his car was also absent. All this Mafia rubbish was affecting her brain. She started to worry that something might have happened to him. Then she gave herself a nip. "Stupid woman." Maybe Charlie was right, she was becoming obsessed. If anything had happened, he would have rung her. If there had been an accident the police would have been banging on the door. She went for a shower, then remembered that she needed to be at her mother's house at 8-30 for the skip delivery. Graham had always had trouble getting out of bed, their mother was used to shouting upstairs 'Graham is your back stuck to the sheet again?' So, she should have to be at the house and the visit to the library could wait. Besides, they might also hear from the Italian Embassy, and it could very well be a mistake.

As she ate breakfast a thought flashed across the screen of her mind. Perhaps those papers had been in the desk before her parents bought it? 'Damn' she thumped the table, no that was no good, her mother told her about Leggio, she didn't know Janice would find that hidden drawer, by sheer chance. If they had nothing to do with her, she wouldn't mention them, because she wouldn't know they were there. She was getting into a real mess. She decided that the best thing to do was to get ready and go to the house, clear her head once again and get on with her life!

By the time she arrived, she was annoyed, the skip had already been delivered, plonked on the front lawn. The annoyance made way for a chuckle when she thought about how her mother would react were she still here. Boy she would have been furious.

"How dare you put that monstrosity on my finely manicured lawn!" she would have screamed.

Graham had not arrived, she laughed again recalling the thought of before. When he came, she should tease him about it. She decided to continue in the lounge, the desk was still too empty. So much paper, half of it was rubbish, junk mail advertising flyers, which should have gone straight to the dustbin as soon as they got through the mailbox. But in the middle of it all were little nuggets. Pictures they had painted as children, birthday cards, all well wrapped in tissue paper. More and more memories. There were photographs of people she had no idea who they were. Wedding photographs from the 1920s. They were obviously relatives on Archie's side. There was no way they could be on her mother's side of the family. There were council tax bills, gas bills, almost every bill you could think of. All in their own envelope with the date written on the front. Well, their mother had been a legal secretary. Huh, the irony that she worked for the law and Leggio worked against it. She wondered if her career had been deliberate, so she could metaphorically "spit in his face". Janice wondered what her mother really felt about this man, was it a silly encounter, she slept with him because she feared that if she refused, he could kill her. From what she had read about this man so far, it was all too real a possibility. Then she had a cold shiver down her spine. The only thing she had never thought of before. Had he raped her mother? Was this the reason she was thrown out of the house, forced to leave and go to Naples, then again forced to seek refuge elsewhere? For the first time, Janice felt some compassion for her mother. This may explain why she once told her: 'I never asked for you nor wanted you', when they had one of their mother and daughter fallouts. She looked at her watch, it was almost 1-30 and still no sign of Graham.

When he did arrive, she was furious with him; well, it was Charlie who she was cross with, Graham was just there to get both barrels.

Not what he expected when he walked in through the door.

"Where the hell have you been, my God I have enough to worry about with Charlie AWOL, then you don't even show, what was I going to think?"

"Hey sis chill, it's not my problem Charlie stayed out all night, I can come and go whenever I want, it's not a job you know."

"Don't get clever with me..."

"I know, but..."

They were interrupted by Charlie's arrival.

"What the hell is going on?"

"Watch yourself Charlie, she will be having a go at

you in a minute." Graham excused himself and went to the garden for a smoke. He was used to being banished outside; Mother would never let him smoke in the house.

"He's right, where the hell have you been all night and a half a day. You've never been out like this before. Not a word. I was worried sick."

"Well, sorry honey, but it takes some getting used to finding out you've married into the Mafia."

"Oh, for God's sake, that's where you were bingeing on films about gangsters, which is the American Mafia not 'Cosa Nostra'."

"Oh, begging my pardon sorry. So now you are an expert on the various Mafia factions after reading some books. When you first told me this tripe, I went along with it, Graham agreed, because we both knew your grief at the loss of your mother hadn't manifested itself yet. But he's taking control of your life, this Italian bastard is driving a wedge between us."

"Sicilian," Janice corrected him.

"See, there you go, who gives a shit if he is Italian or bloody Sicilian? I have had it. I need to leave for a while, I can't cope with all this, not with the pressures of work on top of this."

"But Charlie, I need you, I need your support." There was an almost pathetic girlish tone in her voice.

"No, I'm sorry I have to go." Charlie got up and began to walk to the door, Janice pulled on his arm trying to stop him from going, but he was adamant. There was such a commotion that it brought Graham rushing back into the house; he found Charlie gone and his sister sobbing on the floor.

Four

IT HAD BEEN three months since that fateful day at the home of her late mother. She had not seen or heard from Charlie; she had tried to call his parents, but of course they had gone ex directory, because the operator said the number was no longer in use. She tried to write, but the letters were never answered. Even when she contacted his office, they said he wasn't available. Janice had begun to accept her marriage may well be over.

The sale of their parents' house came to an end, Graham had been true to his word, once he paid the inheritance tax, he gave her half. Thanks to his generosity, she was able to realise her dream of opening her own art studio. She had always liked to paint since childhood, when her favourite aunt bought her a painting by numbers for Christmas, she went from that drawing in freestyle, to painting her first oil on canvas; she had always preferred oils, feeling that watercolours were wishy washy.

Charlie decided to return and hit the front door bell. A young man came out of the kitchen with a T-towel in his hand and answered the door.

"Excuse me, you can't come in here!" said the young man looking down the hall.

"I think it should be excuse me, who the hell are you and what are you doing in my house."

"Well, if it's any of your business, I'm allowed by Janice to be here."

"My wife you mean."

"Oh, you must be the absent husband Charlie isn't it?" the young man turned and returned to the kitchen.

Charlie made most of the time being alone and looked around, she had decorated, not bad; he could hear a conversation emitting from the kitchen. A few moments later the young man returned.

"Janice is on her way home."

"Where is she?" Charlie asked as he invited himself into the lounge and noticed that there were pictures of Leggio everywhere; it was hard to miss them there were so many.

"At her studio."

"Oh, she finally opened one, good for her, explains all the paintings, still obsessed with the Mafia, right?"

"No, she has moved on."

"Yes, I can see that, talk about cradle snatching" said Charlie, turning and looking at the young man up and down.

"In case you're wondering, I'm Gavin. I'm going to go get some coffee."

Charlie took a picture of Leggio, a right baby-faced mobster. He felt slightly melancholy when he saw that still pride of place above the fireplace was their wedding photograph. He gave a deep sigh and sat down on the couch. When Gavin came back with coffee, Janice stormed in.

"Take it you're not glad to see me then? Scared I could get in the way?"

"What, you just swan back in here, and expect me to fall at your feet. I've grown up a hell of a lot since you walked out on me."

"I went on a kind, a sort of sabbatical, that's all."

It wasn't a good thing to say, Janice marched across the room and slapped him hard on the face.

"Aunt Janice" Gavin pulled her away.

"Aunt?" Charlie said getting over the shock of the slap.

"Yes, idiot, Gavin is not my toy boy, he is my cousin, he is studying here at the agricultural college, so I said he could stay with me and save money on having to pay for student accommodation."

"Look, I'm sorry, so I jumped to the wrong conclusion, it's just when you come home and find a kid in your house. What was I going to think?"

"Oh yes, the house, I paid the mortgage, I had it valued, and your half of the value is sitting in my savings account. So, I can transfer it whenever you want, I'd rather do it before I start sorting out the divorce."

Charlie looked visually stunned, that was the last thing he expected; he knew she'd be furious with him, but a divorce.

"This is adult stuff I'm going to go to my room, I need to plan an essay." Gavin wanted to get out of that room as fast as his legs would take him. He didn't want to be caught in the crossfire – he had enough of that at home.

"Look Gavin I'm really sorry; it just wasn't what I expected. I should have let you explain."

"All right Charlie, all sorted now."

They must have talked for hours. Charlie did most of it trying to explain that he found everything so hard to deal with. He was so sure that she would want to go to Sardinia to try to see Leggio, then perhaps also to Sicily to try to find her mother's relatives. It wasn't until he left that he realised they could have done it together.

He stayed for the evening meal and had a long chat with Gavin about the agricultural industry, and how the small farmer could avoid being swallowed up by the so-called mega farms. It got late and Charlie had drunk a couple of beers while chatting, so though not happy about it, she said he could stay, but in the guest room. She had given Gavin the spare room because it was larger and meant he could have a desk in there to work undisturbed. They both lay awake thinking about each other, and if their marriage was salvageable, or as the saying went "had too much water passed under the bridge"? Charlie, for his part, knew he had to accept Leggio was in their lives at present, so he had to bite the bullet and confront it. In the end tiredness got the better of both and they fell asleep.

Janice panicked when she finally woke up, realising that she had forgotten to set the alarm. Then, when you work for yourself, there's no one asking you why you're late for work. The odd late start wasn't a problem unless it started to become a habit. She was disappointed when she came down that Charlie had already gone; why did he

38

feel the need to sneak out, after all they were still married, he could have stay for breakfast. It would have given them a chance to talk: did they get divorced or wipe the slate clean and start over? Did she really want a divorce? Charlie gave the impression that he didn't want one.

Once in the studio she tried to focus on a painting she was working on, but it was no good. She put it aside, and before she knew it, she was painting Charlie. That crooked smile he seemed to have, that twinkle in his brown eyes, which was one of the first things she had noticed about him. How she felt a beat in her stomach when he smiled at her across the room. It was a housewarming party, Charlie had been the architect, she had always thought there had been a hint of match making from her brother, but she had not complained; for her it was almost love at first sight. Her thoughts were interrupted by the ring of the doorbell as a delivery man entered with a huge bouquet of red carnations.

"Mrs Richards?" he asked, holding out the flowers for her to take.

"Yes, thank you, they are beautiful."

"Oh, I never chose them, just my job to deliver them." He smiled and left.

She pulled out the little card but didn't understand the message.

"A touch of home" signed C.

A little confused, she realised they were from Charlie, but what did the message mean; she had no idea, and why carnations and not roses? Did he think roses would make him look too pushy under the circumstances?

She didn't have a vase to put them in, so she took them to the sink in the storeroom, put the plug in the sink and added some water; they would be fine there until she went home. Then she went back to her painting of Charlie, she had just started adding oils when the flowers had arrived. She sat on her stool and looked at his face staring at her from the canvas. She began to get tearful. They had fallen in love so deeply almost immediately. There hadn't been a long engagement, they just wanted to get married so they could be together. Of course her mother had poured scorn on this, but they ignored her and had just carried on. She paused momentarily, brushing a tear from her cheek; she wished her father Archie could have been there to give her away, she had always known him as her father; could it really be true that he wasn't. When he died so suddenly, she had cried for days, she would not have anything to do with anyone, even Charlie seemed unable to console her.

"No!" She shouted aloud.

Archie would always be her father, he was the one who consoled her when her rabbit died, she had loved that rabbit so much, she was heartbroken. It was he, rubbing the cream on her knees when she fell and grazed them. The laughs they shared together, the little chats about mother and how matronly she could be. Such happy memories, he would always be her father; this Leggio was just an intruder, a nobody to her, just a name.

She got back to the job in hand. There was not much time to finish the painting but she was satisfied with the result. As she looked at his face, she realised that the love they shared was too valuable a thing to lose, because of the bloody Mafia, and her so-called father! She had to send an olive branch, but how? Then it came to her, she would put this painting in the window, so if Charlie went passed, he would see it.

Charlie was at his desk trying to think about where he was going to stay since it was obvious now that going home wasn't an option. Especially when she was talking about divorce. He cursed her late mother, what the hell had been wrong with her, because she dredged long-forgotten memories up. Was it just to spite her daughter one last time? Had she really hated her with such a passion, then if what she said was true, maybe it was understandable? Yet his conscience told him it was wrong to blame a child for the parent's crimes. His thoughts were interrupted by the intercom.

"Call Mr Richards – your brother-in-law."

"Graham, nice to hear a friendly voice, how's it going?"

"Janice said you were back from the wilderness; you free for a catch up, I dare say you need a place to stay?"

"Yes, the welcome mat at home is turned over." He tried to make a joke of his situation.

"Hey, you must come and stay with me, look, can I meet you for lunch about 1, at the Coffee Met?"

"Great stuff. I have some calls to chase but see you then."

Janice arrived home shortly after 5-00, Gavin was watching TV.

"Hi Janice, I put your mail on the dining table."

"Thank you, what would you like for tea?"

"Whatever you're having will be fine for me," Gavin replied.

She went to look at the mail, flipping through it, mostly junk mail, then saw the logo on the starchy white envelope, and that now-frequent knot twisted in her stomach.

41

It had been so long that she had forgotten about it until now. Charlie's name was on the envelope, but since he wasn't here, and it was about her, she had no problem opening it.

There were two letters, the first letter from the Italian Embassy itself, apologising for taking so long to respond. The second letter was on headed notepaper from Palermo. She felt her hands begin to tremble; she wanted to read them? She dropped both letters on the table and pulled out a chair and then sat down. It had been such a good day; she had started to get her head straight, then there were the wonderful flowers.

Oh God the flowers – she had left them in the studio. That was the tea sorted then, she and Gavin would eat out. Then she could pick the flowers up on their way home. They ate at the steak house, her treat. Gavin joked about how rare his aunt ate her steak, said it was almost still running around the plate. They had a pleasant evening, but the thought of what Palermo's letter might say, sat heavy in her mind. Meal finished, flowers collected, they made their way home.

Gavin said good night and went to his room, Janice got herself a drink and went back to the letters still where she had left them on the dining room table. The letter that mattered contained an overwhelming admission. The previous euphoria she had felt, once she had begun to believe what her mother had said was true, had long since dissipated, and she was ashamed that she had ever felt in her heart that Archie was not her real father.

But the evidence was now in front of her, a birth certificate, not her's, but her mother's, the father of her mother was named as Salvatore Castania, a farmer.

Mother Audenzia Castania, Russo birth name, address was Corleone, the birth name of the child Margherita. She took a sip of her whisky, almost choking as it glided down her throat. She didn't feel anything, just numbness, the only thing she had hoped for so long now wouldn't be true, unfortunately was. Then she tried to see the bright side, this just said that her mother was Sicilian. The letter did not clarify that Leggio was her father, so perhaps there was hope at the end of this long tunnel. She took the letters and put them in the desk; Graham had allowed her to have their mother's, he said it was old fashioned. She opened the secret drawer and put these two new letters with the other documents. Away from prying eyes. She brought the glass into the living room and huddled on the sofa. Perhaps the only way to find out once and for all was to go to Sardinia to visit the prison. Confront this Mafioso; he would know the truth. Then doubts crept in; her mother left in the first part of the pregnancy; would he have known? Oh God, would the only way to know for sure be via DNA, and would he consent to that?

Five

CHARLIE AND GRAHAM got on like a house on fire. There had been no talk of anything to do with the Mafia. It was almost as if they were reliving their student days. As for Janice it had been two weeks since she received her flowers, she had pressed a couple to put in the frame with their wedding photograph. When she spoke to her brother and mentioned Charlie, Graham quickly changed the subject. Maybe, she thought, Charlie accepted they were going to divorce; might he have a new woman in his life? She couldn't let things slip. Positive action that was what was needed, she would return the gesture and send him flowers. But what to send? Freesias, naa, a bit girly for a guy. Then it came to her violets they were often seen as flowers representing peace, sending them would be like holding out an olive branch. Once the flowers were ordered, she knew she had to focus on her work. She was working on a commission painting a barn owl, almost lost against the background of snowflakes as they fluttered down covering the owl, so it seemed to shine as the sunlight caught its feathers in its rays.

She was just cleaning the brushes when the phone rang, she thought she would let the phone answer the call. It was Charlie, so she rushed to reach for the phone before it hung up.

"Charlie, are you still there?"

"Yes, thank you for the flowers, but violets?" He obviously did not have their meaning.

"Yes, they usually represent peace, like an olive branch".

"Oh, I understand you now, nice touch, does that mean you want peace talks?"

"Yes, because when you sent the carnations, I thought it was a cue, but then you never came back to me, I even put some sort of cryptic message in the studio window."

"The painting is very good, is it for sale?"

"Why do you want to buy it?"

"Yes, you've never painted me before, listen how about a meal tonight, your favourite steak house?"

"No..."

"No?" Charlie replied.

"I mean we eat at home; I can cook and that way we can talk without people eaves dropping."

"Don't do this to me, I was just thinking that things were looking up."

"I'm sorry. Don't worry about gooseberry."

"Oh, Gavin you mean?"

"Yes, he'll be out, or in his room he's got a girlfriend."

"See you at seven."

Charlie put down his phone and punched the air. As

a result, his game of playing it cool seemed to have done the trick.

Janice felt giddy as if this were a first date. She packed up early so she could go to the supermarket, she'd have a roast dinner, Charlie had always loved them. Stop by the butchers for a nice silverside joint. Then home wash her hair and decide what to wear. She hoped that the evening would be a success, that the flame would reignite like it had when they first met and melted into each other's arms. What had been the beginning of a wonderful relationship.

Charlie's thoughts seemed to mirror that of his wife, he too was eager to make a good impression, went to get a haircut, and bought a new shirt, and this time he bought roses. He had to endure being teased by Graham, but he didn't care, suddenly he felt like he had just found out he had been left a fortune. Whatever he did, he must not mention Leggio or the Mafia unless Janice addressed the subject first.

When he arrived, Janice answered the door with her apron on, it was a bit awkward to start with, but the conversation soon flowed freely. He sat at the breakfast bar while she basted the joint and checked the vegetables. Then, when everything was in order, they retreated to the lounge for a drink.

"I have to say I like what you've done, maybe you should be an interior designer."

"Eh you're joking, this is a long way from decorating someone else's house for money. I got most of the ideas from the paint book."

"You shouldn't put yourself down."

"You're so sweet, I'll go check the meat, it will have to

rest for a while, so dinner will be about eight if that's ok."

"It's fine whenever it's ready." He smiled and winked. Then cursed under his breath, what the hell did he do that for?

Janice ignored it and went to take the meat out.

"If there's something I can do; I feel bad that you're cooking for me."

"No Charlie I'm cooking for myself; you're just going to eat some of it. She looked at him po-faced before she burst out laughing.

"Oh, your face, I wish I could have captured that in paint."

"You." He went to her and tried to give her a hug but was rejected.

"Go sit down I'll plate up in here."

Charlie thought it was best not to argue and went to sit at the dining table. It was all very formal, place settings at either end of the table. They ate in silence, Charlie still chastising himself under his breath for his faux pas.

They finished their meal and went into the lounge glass of wine in hand. "I had forgotten how good a cook you are." Charlie tried not to sound condescending.

"Ha you're not a fan of Graham's cooking then; more wine?"

"I'm not sure I should have any more wine driving and all that, then I can always get a taxi. I still cannot get over the fact we both chose the exact same bottle of wine, how spooky is that?"

"No not really, we have always liked the same things, so it's natural we would be aware of what each other likes." Janice walked across to refill his glass, put the bottle on the coffee table and sat down next to Charlie, taking his glass from his hand, she made it quite clear what her intentions were. They fell into each other's arms and kissed with such passion within them, Janice felt she was sinking into a bath of rose petals, as long buried away feelings came rushing to the surface. Suddenly Charlie pulled back and stood up. He gulped the last of his wine before he turned to look at a bemused Janice.

Are you sure this is what you want? He asked fearful of her reply, feeling she may have just been lost in a moment.

"Oh Charlie, I never wanted you to go; you went, you were the one that left, I was frantic, called the police, reported you missing. You just vanished without trace; I had no idea what had happened to you. Your office just said you were away on business. In the end once the police knew what had transpired, they felt you had maybe just taken yourself off to cool down."

Janice was despondent; this was not how she had wanted the evening to end, it was all going wrong, oh God why had she made a pass at him, she should have let him do that, had she messed it all up?

She need not have worried; moments later he sidled up to her, took her hand and pulled her towards the stairs. Like they were two teenagers about to lose their virginity, they rushed upstairs and ripped at each other's clothes falling onto the bed giggling.

Poor Gavin, who was a bit of a wallflower, tried to avoid hearing what was going on across from his room. Eventually frustrated that he had been prevented from sleeping, he turned on the radio connected his earphones and tried to get to sleep like that.

Sunlight crept into the bedroom through a space in the curtains. Charlie turned to see Janice still asleep, it had been one hell of a night. He felt a bit woozy as he sat on the edge of the bed; then they had drunk a lot of alcohol the previous evening, he hoped that wasn't why they ended up lost in the passion. He slipped carefully from bed, put on his underwear and shirt and went down for an aspirin and a glass of water.

He felt quite embarrassed when he entered the kitchen to see Gavin at the counter making toast.

"Oh, I'm so sorry I didn't expect you to be up yet," Charlie said trying to put the young man at ease.

"It's ok it is your home, after all," came the answer. Forgetting that his aunt had bought him out. Feeling uncomfortable Gavin said he would take his toast to his room, and it looked like he could not get out of the kitchen fast enough.

Charlie decided to surprise Janice with breakfast in bed, he boiled two eggs; he knew just how she liked them. Then he would – he had done this many times before. He made toast and finally put on a bowl of cereal with ice cold milk. He was just going to take the tray up to her when his plan was thwarted. Janice arrived fully dressed looking as if she had no hangover unlike him.

"Was this for me? Oh, that's so nice, but I usually stop by the deli on the way to the studio." She could tell by his reaction that he looked hurt.

"No problem, I'll sit at the dining table and enjoy." She had not meant to sound sarcastic, but that's how it came out. She took the tray from Charlie and left the kitchen. It was wonderful; as she expected, the eggs were cooked just as she liked, butterless toast and a pot of Earl

Grey. Charlie had brought the paper for her, she looked at that while she finished her tea, then took the tray to the kitchen. It was then that she saw that Charlie's car was gone, a piece of paper held on the refrigerator door by one of the magnets.

'Last night was wonderful, like old times, but I think considering the amount we drank, we probably just fell into bed, had we both been sober I think it's doubtful it would have happened. I don't want to lose you, I love you, I hope we can overcome this impasse. I thought it was best to go, you know where to find me now, if you want us to be together again.' Charlie signed it with a smilie face blowing kisses.

Janice burst into tears, holding the note against her face so she could smell his scent waft up her nose as she sniffed the paper.

"Janice, are you ok?" Gavin asked as he came into the kitchen with his breakfast things.

"Oh yes, I'm fine, just a little melancholy. Are you getting ready for college, you're early?"

"Yes, we are going on a trip to see some kind of fish farm, it has a special name, I'm sorry I don't remember."

"It's ok honey, you have a good day. I'd better get organised."

"Bye then," Gavin said that as he walked into the hallway and took his duffel bag.

Janice now alone in the house, took herself back to her bedroom, she lay on the bed, she closed her eyes and relived the previous night; the passion had been so intense, this had not only been sex, there had been a deeper meaning. A rebirth of their love for each other. She jumped off the bed, ran downstairs as if her life depended on it, picked up the phone and dialled Charlie's office.

"Good morning, Architects by Design."

"Can I talk to Charlie please?" She tried to keep calm, but it wasn't easy.

"Who's calling please?"

"His wife." Saying it was too much and she began to cry again.

"Just putting you through now." The receptionist was anxious not to draw attention to the fact that Janice was crying.

"Janice?"

"Oh Charlie please come home."

"Ahh honey, don't cry I'll be right there."

"Ok." Janice took a deep breath and tried to compose herself. She wiped the tears from her face, went and sat in the dining room so she could see when Charlie's car was coming up the driveway.

It was a long wait for her husband, what seemed like an hour was only about 20 minutes if that. As soon as she saw the car enter the driveway she rushed to the front door. Charlie barely had a chance to get out before she threw herself at him.

"Wow steady on Janice, can't be so bad, is it Graham?"

"Yes, I mean no, it's not Graham, it's me, I realised this morning that I love you so much, I don't want you to ever leave me alone again."

"Let's go in and talk about it." Charlie almost sounded as if he was not quite sure that was what he really wanted. Janice had been so wrapped up in what she wanted. She hadn't looked at it from her husband's point of view.

They went to the living room, where Charlie poured

them both a whisky, went to get some ice and returned, not sitting next to Janice as you might expect him to, but in one of the two armchairs.

"So couldn't it wait till later?"

"You just sneaked out, like it was a drunken mistake."

"Come on Janice didn't you read the note?"

"Well yes, of course I did, that's why I rang."

"Yeh ok, fair point. But I didn't think you would over-react like this."

Janice took a long sip of her drink. Suddenly that dreaded animosity once more raised its ugly head.

"I think you should go, before we both say things that we might not really mean."

"Fine but what's with the hot and cold, you need to make up your bloody mind just what it is you want from me," Charlie snapped, banging the glass on the coffee table so hard that it was a wonder it didn't break. He got up and casually walked out, not to his car, but to the garden. He sat on the bench and lit a cigarette.

Janice had another whisky and then went to swill her face. On her return downstairs Charlie sat down once more in the armchair.

"Oh Charlie I'm so sorry, my head is all over the place. I'm so glad you're here, back in this house, I don't want you to leave it again."

"Come here wife, what are you like. I hope you're not going to lock me in the basement?"

"Oh, there's an idea." She said trying to lighten their mood. If she was honest their marriage had always been so, topsy turvy, one minute it was passionate and calm, then like a sudden sandstorm, it would erupt into anger and recriminations.

"Do you know what we should do?"

"What?" Janice sat on the edge of the sofa. Waiting with bated breath. She was hoping he would suggest that they renew their marriage vows. So when she heard Charlie's idea, it was like being slapped in the face with a wet fish.

"A holiday, somewhere far away where it is hot, with sun-kissed beaches and romantic spots."

"A holiday?"

"Yes, what do you think, when was the last time we were away together?"

"But a holiday?" Janice asked.

"What's wrong, just think, we can go to a really romantic place, wherever you want, just please don't say Sicily."

"As if I would want to go there. You choose somewhere, then you can surprise me." Janice tried to look excited, but was devastated that it wasn't what she wanted to hear. Then maybe a holiday was just what she needed and with the man she loved, it could be a second honeymoon.

Six

GAVIN TOLD HIS aunt he was moving out. Not because Charlie had come home, but simply because a friend in college had asked if he fancied moving into the house; one of the other students had moved in with his girlfriend, so it meant there was now a spare room.

HE HAD SNAPPED his friend's hand off. He wasn't sure what damage he was doing to his ears by staying at his aunt's. He had started switching his radio on as soon as he got to bed. Sometimes he felt as if he lived in a brothel, the noise of sex was now almost of daily occurrence.

"Did they never get tired of it?" Then obviously not. He had thought to himself.

It was a few days later when Charlie came into the house after work looking as if he had just found out he had won a lot of money. He found Janice in the kitchen preparing their evening meal.

"Right sweetheart come and sit at the breakfast bar and close your eyes."

"Charlie, I am trying to get the food ready," Janice said putting down the potato she was peeling.

"Come on, come on, it will only take a couple of minutes." He pulled her away from the sink and pulled her across to the chair. Then when he was sure her eyes were closed, he slipped to the hallway table and back into the kitchen, where he held a magazine out in front of her.

"Ok, you can open your eyes now."

She did just that, looking down to see what she was meant to be looking at. Her eyes scanned across the pages from left to right. There in bold type the word 'Sardinia'. She got up without saying a word and went back to the sink, and her job in hand.

"Well, say something." Charlie was rather surprised by her reaction, hoping she would be as excited as he was.

"Sardinia? What the hell, Charlie?"

"So what's wrong with Sardinia, it's not Sicily," he wasn't sure why she seemed so upset.

"Leggio."

"What does he have to do with anything?"

"Are you for real? You want to go to Sardinia because he is there, in prison as you well know."

"So why would that stop us from going there? Hell it is not as if he's going to ask you to pop in and visit, is it?"

"No, I don't care, I'm not going." Janice was adamant.

"You'll have to, it's paid for and if I cancel I won't get a refund."

"Well, go alone, no wait take Graham, it looks like he's your new best friend, I'm sure he'll love a vacation, brothers-in-arms and all that." She threw the potato peeler in the sink, took off her apron and told Charlie he could get his own tea, she was going out.

She got into her car, drove to the nearest phone booth and phoned her friend Penny, to see if she could pop round for a natter. She stopped at the off license and bought a bottle of wine and made her way through the city to Penny's house.

"I'll get you a glass."

"You not drinking?" Janice asked as she handed the bottle over to Penny.

"Oh no, not during the week, need to be bright and breezy for school in the morning."

She came back with the glass and the cork screw.

"So the honeymoon's over then?"

"Oh Penny why does he have to spoil it."

"So, what did he do that's driving you to drink?"

"Sardinia."

"I'm sorry, the island you mean?"

"Yes, he wants to go for a vacation."

"This is a problem? God I wish Paul would want me to take me to some Italian island, well any island come to that, the sea, sun and sand sounds idyllic. Tell you what, I will go to in your place, you can stay here and take care of the kids for me."

The frown Janice directed at her friend left her in no doubt that she had crossed the line.

"Sorry, so why don't you want to go?"

She just repeated the one word she had said to Charlie. In an almost identical way Penny asked the same question Charlie had.

"He wants to go, because he wants me to visit Leggio, to find out if he's my father or not." She had told Penny

57

about him when Charlie had gone for those few months, she needed to talk to someone about it, and she and Penny had been at school together, so it was the natural choice, the only person who she could unburden her soul to, and know it would go no further.

"He never talks to me about him. But Graham says he always asks if he has any idea what I'm going to do."

"Oh, so you think this is an indirect way of pushing you into it?"

"Yeh exactly. At the moment I'm just coming to terms with the fact that not only was my mother not English neither was my father, and I myself am Sicilian. Charlie can't understand that discovering your life until a few months ago was a huge lie takes a while to get used to; as they say, 'baby steps'."

"Here have another drink." Janice held her glass out and Penny topped it up.

"So, what has been decided?"

"I told him point-blank that I'm not going, that if he wanted to go, then he should go, and take Graham his best friend."

"Ouch."

"What angered me more than just being cross was the fact that he was more worried about losing the refund than the fact that he had upset me. He didn't seem to worry about that. Bloody men!"

"Yeh men, we can't live with them, but we can't live without them."

They both giggled, then talked about other girly things. Janice after drinking the whole bottle of wine took a taxi home and said she would collect her car in the morning.

When she got home, Charlie had gone to sleep in

the guest room, so Janice slept alone. For once she was happy with this, she had been the dutiful wife and let Charlie make love to her every night, but it had become mundane and more like a routine than an act of passion. It would be nice to be able to turn off the light and get an uninterrupted night's sleep.

She woke up feeling refreshed and ready to face anything the day threw at her. She showered and dressed, she didn't bother to check if Charlie was still sleeping. She went down to breakfast.

"Morning did you sleep well?" She tried to make conversation with Charlie, who was sitting at the kitchen table flipping through the travel brochure.

"Well, what about you?" Charlie asked.

"Yes thank you. Then the wine at Penny's could have helped."

"You will be pleased to hear that Graham has accepted my offer."

"Oh Charlie, please don't let's start the day like this, what's going on with us? We never used to fight like this."

"No well things have changed, haven't they?"

"But we can get around it."

"Ignoring the huge elephant in the room?"

"It's going to take time," Janice said on her way to get the milk.

"Time, time? It has been five months, it takes time if you bury your head in the sand and you won't deal with it."

Charlie got up and left the kitchen; she heard the front door close and he was gone.

Janice picked up her car from Penny's and went to her

studio. She hadn't been open for long, when two well-dressed gentlemen came in.

"Miss Castania?" one of them asked.

Janice felt a chill as a shudder shot down her spine. The man spoke with an Italian accent.

"I'm sorry, my name is Janice Richards," she replied in a muffled voice.

"Yes, but your original name is Gigliola, your mother was Margherita yes?" He looked at one of her paintings.

"Who are you?"

"Oh, please don't be afraid, we're here to ask for your help," the other younger gentleman said.

"Do you mind if I sit down? My knees are not good."

"Yes of course; if you are here for my help and it is with a painting, I am not really a restorer as such."

"Oh, nothing to do with art, it's more financial in nature."

"I'm sorry, this is an art studio, not a bank or a loan company."

The two gentlemen then told Janice that the word in Italy said that she was well connected, linked to a 'man of honour'. They ran a small pizzeria and had a slight cash flow problem. They had been told she could help. Janice felt sick, her stomach seemed to have tied itself into a knot.

"I'm sorry you were misinformed, so please, I don't want to be rude but please leave now." She went to the phone and picked up the handset as if she were going to call someone, maybe the police?

"We're sorry you can't help us, come Luigi, we're wasting our time here."

"But Charlie said she would help us."

"Charlie!" Janice almost shouted his name.

"Yes, he often comes to our pizzeria with another man Graham."

"Oh, he does, well, he shouldn't have said anything to you."

"Is it true?" Luigi asked.

"Is what true?"

"That you are the daughter of Don Leggio?"

"Come on Luigi." The older man seemed as if he did not want to hear her answer. He stood at the door, and gestured once again to Luigi, who waited for her reply. None was forthcoming, so he walked up to his companion. As he was about to leave, he turned around and looking directly at Janice in the eye said.

"Don Leggio will be disappointed that you chose not to help us."

As soon as they left, Janice rushed to the door, double locked it and turned the open sign to closed and put down the blind. She was physically trembling, close too tears. Then the anger erupted inside and she marched to the phone.

"Good afternoon Architects by Design."

"Please, can I talk to Mr Richards?"

"Who's calling please?" asked the receptionist.

"Mrs Richards."

"Oh, I'm sorry, he's with a client right now, shall I ask him to call you back?"

"No, it will keep," Janice replied in a harsh tone. As she put down the phone. She wondered what the receptionist thought of her; one minute she rang and was in tears, the next she was ringing and sounded as if she wanted to bite her husband's head off.

She started to redial, then decided that a face-to-face confrontation was in order. She couldn't talk to Charlie, but she could damn well confront her brother. She sat down and put the kettle on. A cup of tea, was called for to help calm her down, she was so angry that her blood pressure must have sky rocketed. She needed to be calm when she got there, it was no good going in screaming at Graham, he would just clam up.

Seeing Graham was a waste of time; he made it clear that he had no idea what his sister was talking about, and when she left she decided he could be telling the truth. He had never been very good at telling lies and when they were young, his ears used to get very red when he told a lie. Graham had noticed that she seemed to stare at him curiously, so she had to avert her eyes from him. She would have more luck with Charlie, after all Luigi, or whoever he really was, had already grassed him up. It would be difficult for him to talk his way out of this.

Janice decided rather than scream and shout that she would play the long game, not mention it to Charlie and see how he reacted. She was sure Graham would have rung to warn him. So she prepared the evening meal, set the table and was watching the news on TV with a cup of tea when Charlie came in.

"Hey, there, had a productive day?" she asked as he came into the lounge.

"Yes, fine thanks the building inspector was happy with the changes he had asked for."

"Good, tea will be about 30 minutes if you want a quick shower." Janice was surprised that she acted so cool and collected, when the little voice in her head was screaming to be let out. A rather puzzled Charlie took himself upstairs as she had suggested to take a shower.

They exchanged chit chat while they ate, and then after the dishwasher was filled, they settled down to watch TV. They sat cuddled together engrossed in a wildlife documentary when the bell rang.

Janice heard talking at the front door, then Charlie invited whoever it was in. The shock when she saw who it was.

"This is…" He never got to finish the sentence.

"Luigi," Janice said, getting up.

"Mrs Richards please forgive this intrusion, but my father is so upset, he was sure you would help us. I had to try once more."

"Sit Down Luigi, Janice and I will go make some coffee, Janice." Charlie made a gesture that she should follow him into the kitchen.

"How did you know his name?" Charlie asked.

"Oh, I never said, he and his father walked into the studio this morning, they wanted to know if as an artist they could commission me to make a mural. In the pizzeria."

"Oh I see." Charlie had no idea what the hell was going on, so he took the coffee back to Luigi. Followed by his wife who had seen the confusion all over her husband's face.

"No, when I saw Luigi, he came to see me because he needed money."

"Yes, the Italian community is very close. We were sure you would help," Luigi replied.

"Why do you need money?" Janice suddenly felt a kind of aura developing over her, it seemed that she had been sucked into a different kind of reality.

"We have a family run business, we had to switch suppliers, so prices for cheese, tomato paste went up, it's hard with so many competitors, we are losing business, it's hard to maintain cash flow."

"But surely you can get cheaper cheese, tomato paste from the supermarket, you go in there, I see row on row of tin tomatoes. Why not cut costs using them?"

Luigi gasped. "No no, we are authentic Italians, our products must come from Italy."

"There's an English saying 'sometimes you have to cut the cloth accordingly'"

"Janice, Luigi will not understand that!" Charlie was getting a little annoyed with his wife. She had a lot of money why didn't she just help the poor guy and his family out!

"How did you know about my father? That as the daughter of a 'man of honour' I would choose to help you?"

"The people of Palermo say it's true, Don Leggio has a daughter in the UK. Word comes from Sicily that you live here."

"Ok let's move on, you want me to lend you money. How much and what do I get out of the deal?" She sipped gently from her cup, she was finding this meeting rather exhilarating.

"We need two thousand pounds. We expect you to charge us interest yes?"

"No, I want more, a part of the business."

"What, Janice this man is my friend." Charlie was outraged.

"Ok, you give him the money. Look, Luigi, go talk to your family about it, then call me in a couple of days."

Janice got up and left the room, leaving both men sitting there stunned.

When Luigi had left, with a cheque for two thousand in his pocket, given to him by Charlie, Charlie went to the kitchen where Janice was emptying the dishwasher.

"What the hell was all that about?"

"That's what you wanted, isn't it? Me to come out as the Mafia boss's daughter. I thought I might as well play the part."

"No, no Janice you're getting carried away with it again. This is not what I wanted."

"Huh you expect me to believe that, you told him who I was, all these Chinese whispers in Palermo, how would they know my name, my mother's name..." Suddenly she had a horrible thought.

"Are you ok Janice?"

"Oh my God, the letter."

"Letter, what letter? You're not making sense."

She sat at the table and put her head in her hands. Then she went on to tell Charlie about the letter from the Italian embassy, and the one that had come from Palermo. Luigi was right, someone had been a party to or had heard through the grapevine, of an English woman who wanted to know about a family in Corleone, as she was trying to discover the family of her late mother. That was it then; the secret was no longer a secret, so she might as well stop pretending and be who she really was.

Seven

TUESDAY ARRIVED AND it was time for Charlie and Graham to embark on their holiday in Sardinia. After checking a few days earlier if Janice had changed her mind. But she had still been adamant that she did not want to go. She offered to drive them to the airport, but Charlie said he preferred to take his car, so when they returned they could get home under their own steam and not depend on public transport.

Janice had a lot to occupy her while the boys were away. She had offered to decorate Gavin's room in the house he was sharing. The décor was terrible, all chintzy not the kind a young man would want. Not only that, but after her little white lie to Charlie as to how she came to know Luigi, she had decided that she should advertise that she could make murals on commission. It had been a prudent move, only a day later a couple had entered the studio and asked her if she was willing to paint a wall in their dining room.

With all this to occupy her mind, the days passed so quickly that she had almost no time to think about Charlie and Graham and what they might be getting up to with all that sea and sun. She hoped Graham would find himself swept away by some young woman, he hadn't told her anything about his current girlfriend. She hadn't actually seen them together in quite some time and he never mentioned her in conversation, so maybe it was all over. A new lady in his life, even if it were just a holiday romance, would just be the tonic he needed.

It was a couple of days before the two were due home when she had a disturbing phone call.

"Janice, it's Charlie."

"Oh hello good of you to call me, I hope you're having fun. Graham Having fun?"

"That's just that I'm afraid, a little bit too much."

"What do you mean?" Janice felt the cold shiver right down her spine that you usually got when you knew bad news was coming.

"He fell off the wagon, look, I don't have much time, we're at the airport, I'll take him home to stay with him till the morning; can you arrange for him to go to the clinic. Or if they don't have room to find somewhere else."

"Oh my God Charlie, what the hell happened?"

"I'm sorry I have to go." All she heard then was the dead line.

Janice put her head in her hands. She blamed Charlie for this, he should have looked after Graham. Then common sense kicked in, he wasn't Graham's jailer, he couldn't be with him 24/7. Maybe it was Graham's fault, he let his guard down, but he'd been on the wagon for over a decade. Even with the mother giving him grief, he had not wavered, and now he had returned to that darkness at the mercy of the demon he had kept at bay for so long.

It was a long night, she didn't sleep much, and she was up before seven. She searched her old address book to find Graham's old counsellor's name and phone number. Hoping he hadn't moved away to work elsewhere. It might be he could have retired, it had been ten years since Graham last saw him. She gave a deep sigh, ten years, not a single drop had passed his lips so what had gone wrong now? Perhaps their GP might be able to help her understand. Was it their mother's death, or even the fact that she might just be his half-sister; he was also struggling with what their mother had said, but he didn't want to burden her with his problems. It was all such a bloody mess. She made tea, and thought about what could be done to get Graham back into sobriety.

"You're awake, how's your head?" Charlie asked Graham as he approached the bed with a strong cup of coffee.

"You have to ask?"

"Here, drink this and take a couple of these, they should help you, mind you, some experts say that the a glass of water is just as good as taking painkillers for a headache."

"I'll go with the tablets." Graham sat up, he was, trembling and almost added to his troubles when the cup slipped, luckily for him the spilled coffee fell on the duvet.

"Janice knows?"

"Yes and no, I did not go into details, I will explain everything when we reach the clinic."

"Clinic oh no Charlie not that bloody place."

"I'm sorry, but you can't go cold turkey by yourself, and Janice and I aren't experienced enough to help you get through it."

"Oh God..." Graham barely had time to put down the coffee before leaning over the bed and vomiting all over the sheep's skin.

It was a relief when Charlie heard the phone ringing, at least now he had an excuse to leave the bedroom. It was as he expected Janice.

"889846"

"Charlie, it's Janice. How is he this morning?"

"Trembling like an earthquake, and he just brought back most of the coffee I made him."

"Right I'm coming, luckily they have a room available in Oakfield. As I thought, his former counsellor has retired and now lives in France. But his son took control of the client list, so that's fine because he's going to know Graham's medical history. See you in a while, give him my love."

"I will."

Janice picked up the bag, the keys to the car and with a heavy heart headed for her brother's flat. When she arrived he was asleep, so she left him be. Going instead to give her husband the third degree.

"Well, let's hear it then?"

"Tea first of all?" Charlie asked meekly.

"No, I just want to know how it is after ten years on the wagon, never a hint that he might fall off, he leaves with you and within four days, he succumbs."

"You won't believe it, but it was a tragic accident."

"Tragic, oh yes, very tragic."

Charlie went on to explain about the two British men they had met at a beach party. They started touring the resort together. Visiting places of interest, they rarely went to a bar. So there was no problem until their holiday was over. They insisted they all meet for a farewell drink. That's when it went wrong. Charlie had been drinking rum and coke, Graham just coke. This way he avoided any embarrassment for Graham.

The problem was that he went with Phil to the bar, but he needed to use the bathroom, when he came back the drinks had been served, he asked which was the rum and coke, so Graham didn't get the wrong drink. Phil seemed flustered but pointed to the nearest glass to Charlie. What he didn't know until it was too late, Phil had decided that the bartender should put the rum in both cokes. Well, that's it, a sip and it was game over. He had tried to get Graham to leave with him, but Phil and his partner Tim gave him a hard time. Graham himself was getting aggressive. He stayed and went on to just coke and tried to swop the glass, but it wasn't any good. So here we are now. The other two left early the next morning, no idea what they had done.

Janice knew in her heart, that what she had just heard must be true, it was too feasible to be a made-up tale, so that Charlie could cover his own back. The way he had spoken the sorrow in his voice, of course they were so loyal to each other, Charlie would never do anything like that. She got up and gave him a reassuring hug.

"We'd better go see if he's awake, he'll need to shower and get dressed. Oakfield are expecting him after lunch from 1-00 p.m. onwards."

As soon as Graham saw his sister, he cried like a little boy who had lost a precious dog. Between his sobs he kept saying he was so sorry. Janice embraced him so tightly.

"It's ok, Charlie explained everything to me. Soon you'll be on your feet, you've done it once, I've been so proud of you for ten years, and I will be again. We're going to do it all together, all three of us. United as one against the demon drink."

Charlie turned and frowned he didn't like what she was suggesting. Graham, meanwhile, had stopped crying long enough to give a brief smile. He pulled himself together, got out of bed and went to the bathroom.

She and Charlie went to wait downstairs while Graham got ready to join them.

"So what happened while we were away. More visitors wanting money from the Mafia Princess?"

"What? Well, if you want to talk about things like that at a time like this. I got a painting, you will never guess from who?"

Charlie pulled a face and shook his head.

"That bastard only paints!"

"Sorry Janice, you've lost me, a lot of people paint."

"Leggio, he's only an artist."

"Wow, and so are you, that has to mean something."

"That lot in Palermo, they sent it, apparently he spends his time painting, writing poetry. Can you imagine a man that gets a gun out and kills you if he doesn't like your tone of voice, writes poetry!"

"Yeh I think it's bizarre. So, what did you do with it?"

"Oh the painting, well, there was no way I was having

it in my studio, I took it to Luigi. Who I have to say was like me reluctant to take it. Oh he would take my money, oh sorry Mafia money, but not a painting."

"So, where is it now?"

"Hanging on the wall in the pizzeria. I told Luigi that Don Leggio might be a little upset if he found out that Luigi had rejected such a personal gift. He tried to be clever and say as it was sent to me, I might be the one he would be upset with."

"So he took it then?"

"I told him not to be so arrogant with me, or the boys might be round."

Their conversation came to a sudden end with the arrival of Graham, suitcase in hand, jacket over his arm.

"I'm ready, no need to pack; the case was still full from the holiday."

"Men! You're really going to need clean underwear, socks, I'm going to run upstairs and get some."

Janice left the two men and went back upstairs, as she was looking through the chest of drawers for some socks and some underwear she noticed a photograph. She took it out and looked down, confused by what she saw. Her thoughts were interrupted when Charlie shouted that she needed to get a move on. She hastily put the photo in the drawer, took some socks, opened a second drawer, took some underwear and made her way back downstairs. When she opened the suitcase she pulled out the dirty laundry and replaced it with clean. That done they all got in Charlie's car and headed off for the clinic.

When they got to the clinic, Graham had a bit of a wobble; he didn't want to go inside, afraid once in there that he would never leave again. If only he knew how true that would be. After some coaxing by his two companions, they managed to get him in.

He was pleasantly surprised; gone was the old dowdy Victorian décor and now it was light and airy; maybe it wouldn't be so bad after all.

Graham was shown in his room by an efficient-looking polite nurse, only in a place like this they weren't wearing a uniform, it was a more casual sense of dress. While Graham was settling in, Charlie was just about to tell the counsellor why Graham had fallen off the wagon when he was stopped. It was up to Graham to tell the counsellor what had happened. Charlie was a little confused how could Graham tell him why he had started drinking again after so long. Graham had a drink, got drunk period. The counsellor explained how everything worked, then said he needed a private word with Janice. So she and the counsellor went to his office.

She was about to join her brother and Charlie when she heard them not arguing as such, but their voices were a little raised. So she stayed outside to see if she could gather information from their heated discussion.

"I have to tell her Charlie, I can't go on like this. She's my sister, after all."

"For fuck's sake grow up, it's too late, now. You're committed, don't blow it for me now." Charlie sensed that someone was listening.

"You must be strong, you can overcome this…" he was interrupted by Janice entering the room.

"Is everything ok?"

"Yeh Graham is still blaming himself, I told him it was due to those two knob-heads. He just needs to focus on getting better. We will support him won't we Janice?"

"Janice?"

"Oh sorry miles away." There was something not quite right about all this. Maybe Charlie was being a little economical with the truth. Then there was that photograph, she needed to take a proper look at that.

"Well, we will leave you to settle in, get some rest. I'll pop in tomorrow, come on Charlie let him sleep." She made a gesture they should go.

Charlie drove his wife back to Graham's apartment so she could get her car, he left her and said he would see her at home. She didn't want to look suspicious by saying she had to go to the apartment, so she just got into her car and waved at Charlie as he drove past.

She was happy to be home and have her slippers on, she sat down and tried to decide what to cook for tea. Looking at the clock, she wondered why Charlie wasn't home yet, after all he had left before she had even started her car. It didn't matter he would 'be here when he was here'. For the first time in hours, she managed a slight smile, she never understood why people said that, it was a stupid thing to say. Her mind went back to the photograph, she felt that maybe she was reading too much into it. She could have a better look tomorrow.

Back at the clinic, the counsellor was eager to start with Graham. They talked about his life, about the death of his mother and how it might have affected him? When Graham explained how he ended up blind drunk, the counsellor was somewhat taken aback. His take on it was simple: Graham had not fallen of the wagon, he had been pushed. This would make a huge difference to his treatment, and he wouldn't be in the clinic as long as they first thought he would be. This cheered Graham up no end and he even said he felt ready to eat something.

When Charlie came back he found Janice in the kitchen, there were several empty bottles of wine on the draining board.

"My God, you're not turning to drink?" Charlie said only jokingly, but the look his wife gave him when she turned around made him realise it was an insensitive thing to say and apologised. Janice said she didn't want to cook, and fancied a big haddock from the local chippie. Charlie said it was a good idea. While he was on his way to the fish shop, Janice set the table and took the empty wine bottles and put them in the recycling bin.

They ate their meal in silence, Charlie wanted to have a beer with his, but he thought better not. So he settled for a glass of water. Janice took the empty plates to the kitchen, put the dishwasher on and said she was going for a long soak in the bath.

Once Charlie was sure Janice was out of the way, he took an envelope out of his pocket and looked at the contents, before taking it and putting it in his briefcase; then, making sure it was locked, he took it back into the study.

Eight

ALTHOUGH HE HAD two days off, returning home early, Charlie decided to go to work. He gave Janice a kiss and said he hoped Graham would have had a good night. Did she want him to come to the clinic after lunch? He really didn't want Janice to be alone with her brother. She shook her head. He didn't show her that he was bothered about it.

She finished breakfast, filled the dishwasher, brushed her hair, made sure she had both sets of keys and set off to Graham's flat. She could have a hoover round while she was there. The first thing to do was to look at that photograph. She rushed upstairs and almost ran into the bedroom, pulling the drawer open so forcefully, she almost pulled it on to the floor. She searched frantically through the pairs of socks, but it wasn't there. Maybe it was the next drawer? She looked in there, but there was no sign of it. She began to doubt herself, maybe she had not seen a photograph, only thought she had? She shook her head, it was so bizarre. She kept having this annoying feeling that something was going on, was it to do with Leggio, or was she letting her imagination run riot again? Whatever, she needed to shake a leg.

Once downstairs she checked the fridge, there wouldn't be much in it anyway with Graham being on holiday. She decided to clean it out, and leave the door open so it wouldn't grow mould. After a quick run around with Henry, she then made her way to the clinic, stopping off at the supermarket to get him some magazines to read, and some toiletries.

When she arrived she rang the buzzer to be let in.

"Can I help?" a voice said over the intercom.

"Oh yes. good morning. Mrs Richards to see my brother Graham."

"Er Mrs Richards, I'm so sorry, your brother doesn't want to see anyone."

"But surly Graham will want to see me?"

"No, I'm sorry he said even you, he just wants to be left alone to recover without any more pressure."

"But I have things for him – magazines, aftershave etc."

"I'm coming to get them from you." Moments later a young woman arrived at the door. Janice reluctantly gave the toiletries and magazines to the young lady and left.

The year marched on and before she knew it, Christmas had been and was gone. Graham was still in the clinic, still refusing to see anyone. Janice was worried about her brother, but the counsellor who looked after him said he was fine, doing very well and it would not be long before he could go home. So what happened next was heartbreaking.

It was about 3-00 in the morning when the phone rang. Janice heard it first, but she wasn't sure, so she nudged Charlie to ask if he could hear it. He could and he said he'd go see who it was. Maybe there was a break in at his office or in the studio. Janice waited for him to come back.

Charlie came into the bedroom, she knew straight away something was wrong. She jumped out of bed, and began to dress.

"It's Graham isn't it? Well don't just stand there, tell me," she yelled at her husband.

He looked stunned and slowly sat on the bed. He was trying to think of a way to tell her.

"Janice I can't find an easy way to tell you… so I will just say it, when they went to check on Graham, they found him hanging in his bathroom." He waited for her to react, but nothing happened, she didn't scream, there were no tears, she took off her bra and pants and got back in bed.

"Did you hear what I said?"

"Yes yes yes, I heard you, what do you want me to do?"

At last he thought some kind of reaction. Then it happened she cuddled in her pillow and wept, crying herself to sleep.

Charlie went downstairs and poured a large whisky, my God, what else was going to go wrong? Last year had been a hell of a year, now this year was going the same way. Where did they go from here, Janice already looked as if she was stressed out, this could push her over the edge, and maybe result in her having a nervous breakdown.

A new day dawned but the events of the middle of the night were still very real. This had not been a nightmare, no strange dream, it was fact, it had really happened. First the drink and now he had hanged himself. No one really knew what was going on in someone else's mind.

Charlie could only surmise, he wasn't a psychiatrist, but he guessed something wasn't quite right when Graham refused to see anyone, especially Janice. Had he wanted to protect her from his inner turmoil, but surely that wouldn't have been anything compared to what he left her with now?

He made some camomile tea and gingerly went upstairs. Janice was in the bathroom, her face red, her eyes swollen because she had cried so much; she was dressed, brushing her teeth.

"Honey, what are you doing dressed?" Charlie went to try to hug her, but she pushed him away.

"Oh, so it is like that is it, you're going to blame me. Hell if he hadn't been in the clinic, no doubt you would have blamed Leggio," Charlie snapped, upsetting his wife, who would not allow him to console her.

She just swilled her mouth, turned and glared at him. Before returning to the bedroom, where she sat at the dressing table to put some foundation on to hide her red eyes.

"It is 6-30 in the morning, where are you going that you have to be dressed and wear make up?"

"Where I'm going, you have no idea have you, your parents are still alive. My mother died, the man I thought was my father died, and now almost a year later my brother is dead. You have to ask me where I'm going?" she yelled at him.

"I'm sorry, because I understand, no I don't really, explain it."

"You're really a bastard, right? I'm going to see my brother, hold his hand and kiss his face, and tell him how sorry I am for letting him down, that he thought because he could only be my half-brother, that I didn't really care what happened to him. My mother the whore did this to him, because as a good Catholic she had to get rid of her guilt, or she would end up in hell. All those years she stripped off Graham and I with her sordid little secret. He must have felt so lonely. Doing something like that, when you hang yourself, it means you really want to be dead. You're not looking for attention, you just want to be gone from pain, free of the mental torture life is throwing at you."

It was all too much for Janice and she broke down again, this time she allowed her husband to console her. He gave her the warm camomile and she drank it – that and nettle tea she could drink even when it was cold.

"Oh sweetheart, let it all out, get rid of the anger, you need to grieve for him. You're coming out of the shock. He was a terrific guy we were like brothers when we first did..." Charlie stopped suddenly, almost letting a secret of his own slip then, but he just realised before it was exposed.

"I think I'll go back to bed, for a while I'll try to get some sleep. You're right, it is a little early to go to the clinic."

"He won't be there anyway, they'll have taken him to the morgue at the hospital."

"Oh Charlie, he will be so cold in there, he'll be all alone."

"He won't know anything about it. Here let me help you undress."

He put his wife to bed and covered her, then lay beside her over the duvet until she went to sleep. He would ring the GP later to see if he could get her some tranquillisers to help her deal with this latest tragedy.

Nine

GRAHAM'S INQUEST WAS opened and adjourned to allow the coroner to undertake further inquiries. This added to his sister's concerns. The business with Leggio would come out. At the time the Mafia was everywhere, the Maxi trial of the Sicilian Mafia had begun in a specially built courthouse, within the perimeter of the Prison Ucciardone in the Sicilian capital Palermo. Newspaper, television, radio was everywhere. For the first time Janice got to look at the man her mother had claimed was her father. He was well dressed, with curly grey hair, had a large cigar in his mouth. She felt a strange feeling, both of a sense of loyalty to this old man (after all he was 61 years old), but also a deep disgust that he was as murderous as the books she had read said.

CHARLIE BEGAN TO worry more and more about his wife, she had stopped going to her studio, saying she needed to grieve for Graham. When in truth she just wanted to spend all day reading the papers about the trial. She had also started to have Italian newspapers delivered to them. Taking them to Luigi in the pizzeria. He then translated all the articles concerning Leggio into English. More and more she began to talk about him as if she were now convinced that he was her real father. Gone was that revulsion she had once been so intent on having. She apologised for him, saying that he had grown up in poverty, that he had stolen only to try to improve his life, so he and his siblings had food on the table. But somehow he saw what Michele Navara had and wanted it, but not just a better life, he started wanting power. He wanted to be the same. Perhaps like his brother Carmelo, he was born with a mental disability and suffered from some mental incapacity. In his case, a lack of feelings; he would kill anyone, a priest, an old woman even a child if he had a mind to.

But at the same time this could not be true, he could not have become the 'boss of the bosses' if he had been in any way mentally deficient. After all, he had survived, even now in prison he was still giving orders according to the paper. He was still in charge, letting his two trusted underlings perform the show from the outside. Not since Navara tried to kill him had anyone else tried, his power was so great.

It was a couple of months into the Maxi trial, they were having breakfast when she came out with it.

"I'm going to Sicily," she said in a matter of fact way as she buttered her toast, waiting for her husband's response.

"Are you crazy?" he replied after dropping the knife in shock.

"No, I'm pretty sane, I need to know the truth, the

only way to do that is to go see Leggio."

"You're deluded, as if they will let you into the prison. They're going to laugh in your face. I'd say you'd have a better chance of getting into the vault at the bank of England."

"Not if I go to the papers." Charlie almost choked on his coffee.

"The papers, now I know you have lost it. I don't want my friends, my colleagues, my clients even thinking we are related to the Mafia!"

"But you're not, I am."

"Or so you think, your mother might have been delirious."

"No, I'm sorry, that argument does not hold up, there is a paper trail, evidence not only from the Italian Embassy here, but also from Palermo. It might not prove that my father was Luciano..."

"Oh, so now we're using first names. I've had enough of this, I'm going to work."

"But your breakfast."

"I'm not hungry anymore, I feel sick; I can't believe that you want to go to Palermo, what about the rumours that Luigi told you about, you want to put your neck on the line. You're mad."

"He's still the boss, I'll be fine."

"You're deluded, is this a way to try to block out what's happened in the last year or so, your mother, then Graham. For God's sake Janice get a grip will you." Charlie threw down his napkin and walked out of the dining room.

Janice had some more toast and refreshed her tea, while deciding which newspaper to approach. Italian would be better, it would be more current there with the trial taking place. But which? Giornale De Sicilia or Corrie Del Seira? She went to look at yesterday's paper, then she noticed 'Ansa' and a phone number, it was like a co-operative; its members and owners were the leading news organisations, which was perfect; surely they would have someone who spoke English?

She dialled the number and waited; there was the usual greeting, and a voice asking which language they wanted. Moments later she was talking to a very nice gentleman who wanted to know what she wanted them to report on?

"I think I could be Luciano Leggio's illegitimate daughter."

There was a momentary silence, she could hear the Italian being spoken in the background.

"I'm sorry about that, it took a moment to digest what you said. Do you know who this man is?" The reporter seemed surprised that someone would want to be associated with this Leggio.

"Of course, it was a shock to me, initially I had no idea who this man was; the Italian Embassy in London were very helpful, as were the officials in Palermo."

"Well, you had better give me, some details, my colleague is listening, is that all right?"

"Yes, if I wanted to keep it a secret I wouldn't contact you, especially now with the Maxi trial in Palermo."

Janice told the two journalists the story from the moment her mother gave her confession at the bedside, to where they were now. She told them she wanted to go to Sicily to meet Leggio and maybe meet some of her mother's relatives. They seemed to think it was a good idea. Janice offered to send them copies of the documents to verify what she had said as truthful. But they said it wouldn't be necessary. They had a regional office in Palermo and she should take the documents with her to Sicily. When was she going?

It was her turn to go quiet, she hadn't got that far yet. Then both sides agreed to contact Palermo's office when she was going to travel, then they could agree when to meet.

Janice was like a kid going on vacation. She had never been abroad before, this was her first great adventure, and boy what an adventure. Her attitude towards her mother had changed dramatically in recent months. She felt compassion for her now. A young woman thrown out by her own parents, then the same happens to her again when her uncle discovers she is pregnant. How she must have suffered not knowing what the next day would bring. Then, after the birth of her daughter, she entered a new dawn. She met and married a wonderful Englishman who accepted not only her but also her daughter. No wonder she hid it until she was dying. Was it shame she felt, had she told Archie everything. Or did she keep it hidden from him too? Soon the whole world would know. It could be her new dawn, meeting relatives she had never known existed until now. Or would they disown her as they had done her mother?

In Rome, a hot news story, a new perspective on the 'boss of bosses' was being discussed at Ansa headquarters.

"So Giuseppe you think it's true, or just some crank?"

"That Pietro is a very good question. She is extremely brave..."

"Or very stupid!" Pietro replied.

She did say she had evidence of a birth certificate issued through the Italian Embassy in London. Letters in Sicilian dialect, if it was a scam, would she have known that in Sicily they do not always speak Italian>

"Giuseppe you don't think this is Mafia-related, do you. Some sort of elaborate plot to get to Leggio?"

"It could be, who knows, our colleagues in Palermo will have a better understanding of the politics that surround one of the most infamous Mafiosos to date. I will fax what we have been told, which may initiate some preliminary investigations."

Janice went and got dressed, did her make-up, brushed her hair and headed to some travel agencies. She collected a series of holiday brochures, not only on Sicily but also on Italy. Along with flight details. Once she felt she had enough information, she headed home.

Ten

CHARLIE SAT IN his office, he missed Graham, if he had still been alive he would be asking for his advice. What should he do with Janice? Let her go; he knew the more he spoke against the idea, the more determined she would be to go. So playing along with her would be the right thing to do. But he did not want her to come home in a body bag, dispatched on Leggio's orders, because it was an itch he didn't want to scratch?

"Oh Nora what the hell did you do?" he said under his breath.

Janice called the pizzeria to see if Luigi had any new news from Palermo. People were talking about her and the possibility that she might be Leggio's daughter. He shrugged his shoulders and told her people were too pre-occupied with what was going on in court.

She returned home and settled at the dining-room table, pen and paper in hand. She started looking through the holiday brochure. First the Italian mainland, Naples in particular; she loved boats and had often said that it would be nice to take a river cruise in Europe, perhaps around the Norwegian fjords. With that in mind, she thought it would be nice to travel to Sicily by sea rather than by plane. She was fascinated by the beauty of Naples, the ancient churches, the old architecture, maybe it would be nice to spend a couple of days exploring the city before leaving. It would be foolish to leave the plane and get directly on the ferry. She wondered if Charlie wanted to go; after all, he wanted her to go to Sardinia, so why would he baulk at this idea? It would be so romantic to arrive in Sicily at dawn, if they were travelling overnight. She had spent all afternoon scribbling different flights, cost from each airport; although she had plenty of money in the bank, so she could travel first class if she wished. When Charlie came in, he was less than impressed.

"Oh Janice what is all this?" he asked as he took a brochure, looked at it and threw it back on the table.

"I had a wonderful thought, why not come with me, we can make it a holiday, explore the island together?"

"You're mad. Firstly, this is not about exploring Sicily. Secondly, if you think I want a bullet in the head, you're very mistaken."

"Oh Charlie, this isn't The Godfather," Janice said, trying to get him to agree.

"Damn right there, that was fantasy, this is the reality. You don't mess with the likes of him."

"But he's my father."

"But he's my father, my father. Like I said, you don't know for sure, you assume a lot. Well, if you want to go, go, but there's no way on God's earth that I'm going with you."

Charlie left her and went to the kitchen.

"Oh Janice there's nothing in the oven?"

"It's not a problem, we can have pasta." Moments later Charlie returned to the dining room.

"Bloody pasta, this house is drowning in everything Italian. I'm going to Graham's..." He stopped suddenly; he couldn't go to Graham's anymore, unless he went to talk to him at the cemetery. This too seemed more attractive than having to sit through the evening meal eating bloody pasta as his wife went on and on about Sicily, and anything else she might think was Italian. Next thing he knew she would only allow bloody Italian wine in the house.

Seeing Charlie getting slightly agitated, Janice cleaned up the table and went to prepare their evening meal. She decided against pasta, instead making a Quiche Lorraine, Dauphinois potatoes and green vegetables. She cooled a bottle of South African wine, to get well away from anything Italian. Charlie had gone to shower and change from his suit into something more casual. They ate in the silence that had become more of a habit than an exception. Although Charlie complimented her choice of wine.

She wasn't sure if he was being sarcastic or not, so she thanked him anyway, saying she loved South African Chardonnay. Meal over, Charlie cleared the table, filled the dishwasher, and Janice went to have a bath. Charlie told her he was going to sleep in the guest room. She did not pursue it, not wanting to find herself in the middle of another unnecessary argument.

Charlie had no idea Janice had set the wheels in motion until that fateful message he heard on the answerphone.

"So, when were you going to tell me?"

"Tell you what?"

"Ansa."

"How do you know about them?" Janice braced herself; all they seemed to do nowadays was argue, and it was all going to kick off now.

"Wonderful things answering machines. You ring up, no one is in, so you can leave a message. Did you not see that little red light flashing?"

"They rang, what did they say?"

"I have no idea; once I realised, I erased it."

"You did what, why?"

"Oh Janice, how many times are we going to have this conversation. You're not a spotty-faced teen looking for adventure, rebelling against your parents for laughs. You're almost thirty years old for God's sake. You're supposed to be an intelligent woman, you have read what this man is like, him and his cronies, and you want to swan in there, like a naive student."

"If I remember correctly, it was you who wanted to go to Sardinia."

"Yes, for a holiday, that's all, not because he was there, I thought it would be a nice place to go, that's all."

"Well, I will just have to ring back."

"Like hell you will. I mean it Janice, leave it. These aren't nice people, don't go and think because you're a woman they won't put a bullet in your head. You do not seem to comprehend, that either side could kill you if they want to. Please Janice, I'm begging you to forget this bloody crusade, otherwise it could very well be your death." That said Charlie got up, finished his coffee and left for the office. Leaving Janice to mull over what he had said. It made no difference. A few minutes after Charlie's departure she was straight on the phone to Ansa in Rome.

"Buon giorno, parlare inglese? Si, Gigliola Castania, returning your call." The line went quiet for a few seconds, then the voice came back and he said he had no record of anyone who had made a phone call to someone by that name. Janice said not to worry about it. Whoever it was that rang would no doubt telephone again. She said thank you and hung up. Then she realised her mistake, she should have used her known name, not her birth name. Not only that, but it may not have been Rome but Palermo's office that called her.

She made some fresh tea and cleared the breakfast bar. Then she returned to the dining room to continue planning her trip. She didn't care what Charlie said; she had decided she was going to Sicily. So she needed a one-way flight from Gatwick to Naples. Then a ferry ticket to Palermo. She would return to Gatwick from Sicily. She sipped her tea, and wondered. Was that what her mother had wanted, for her to embark on this journey of discovery? If Graham had been here, she was sure he'd go with her. Graham. She missed him terribly; she thought they would grow old together, that he would get married and have children. She still hoped Charlie might change his mind about not wanting to be a father. There was no chance of that at the moment. She bet herself a wager that he would use it as a bargaining tool to prevent her from going to Sicily. That was the kind of thing he would do. But how did she know he hadn't had the snip?

Her thoughts were interrupted by the sound of the letter box, it was her Italian newspapers. Of course the Mafia trial was all over the front pages; a guy named Tommaso Buscetta, had broken 'Omerta' and was spilling the beans. He was not some small time Mafioso, he was at the top of the pile. His testimony would cause serious damage to the organisation. It didn't matter to Leggio who was destined to stay in prison. Even so it must have seemed like a kick in the stomach, but she had read how Buscetta had lost much of his family during a Mafia turf war. She saw him as a hypocrite, he killed people didn't care about families left behind, but when it happened to his family, well, that was just not on. Even so, it must have taken some guts. Maybe he had a conscience, after all?

It was lunchtime and Janice had a rough idea of how she was going to Palermo, but she still had no idea when she was going. She realised Charlie might try to hide her passport, so she hid it in the desk. She had bought a small leather document holder, at a squeeze it would just fit inside the hidden drawer. So all her paper documents were in the same place.

As she was looking through a box of old documents that had come from their late mother's house, which Graham had taken to his flat, she had found a document confirming that Archie had adopted her. She started to cry because she was sullying Archie's memory, would he have stopped her from going to Sicily, looking for the truth about her mother and Leggio?

She decided she needed some air, so headed to the pizzeria for lunch. On the way she called in at the newsagents and cancelled her delivery of Italian newspapers. It was a small way to appease Charlie. Luigi looked relieved when he saw her enter minus any newspapers. He did not like to offend her, but unlike his elderly father he was not a fan of the Mafia. Once they could be called 'men of honour' but now they were just murderous delinquents obsessed with power and especially money. Every time he looked at that damn painting, he wanted to disfigure it.

"Buongiorno Signora Richards. No papers today?"

"No, there's only so much you need to know. I always find the court case to be so long and drawn out. Soon I'll be in the middle of it as we English say." She gave a laugh, to which Luigi tilted his head and seemed confused.

"I'm sorry Luigi, I shouldn't say that, after all I'm Sicilian," she said rather louder than she meant too, which not only made Luigi feel uncomfortable but raised a few eyebrows with his other customers.

She ordered a Pizza Margherita and laughed again, she was going to eat her mother metaphorically. As she ate and sipped her wine, she looked at the painting. It was almost art deco in style, the geometric shape of the houses. The colours were bright blue sky; orange and yellow coloured the buildings, some houses painted as if they were made of grey yet blue-tinged stones. In the middle of the road leading out of town, there was a man on his horse, well dressed in shirt and tie and a suit, with the classic Italian Cuppula hat on his head. She wondered was this a true reflection of the town? It seemed so quaint. She smiled to herself, now she had to go to Sicily, only to see if Corleone was really like the painting suggested. After some of Luigi's delicious ice cream she finished her wine, paid and left.

"Was that her Luigi?" asked one waiter.

"Yes Giuseppe, that was Don Leggio's daughter. Well, no one knows for sure yet. But in Palermo it is said that they are taking it seriously. So I'd better do the same, and that means, for you and I she is just Mrs Richards."

"Si."

Luigi knew only too well that today people did not broadcast that they were, or had any association with, the Mafia. They had become like the English Free Masons, a kind of secret society. Tensions had been high in the Italian community with the big trial underway in Palermo. There seemed to be a lot of relatives visiting. Because it could just be that they wanted to escape everything.

Charlie had been on site all afternoon, walking around with the building inspector, checking everything in the new building complied with building regulations. But his mind was elsewhere. He was so worried about Janice going to Sicily. The more he read on the news, the more he thought it was the wrong thing to do. Then he realised that he could now bring it all tumbling down, if he talked to Ansa told them that his wife was wrong, that she was obsessive about Leggio, that her mother and brother had died within a year of each other, and she was using this fantasy to try to cope with her grief. Then he felt dejected; could he do such a thing, especially when he knew in his heart that it could be true. The evidence was there, not only that, she had already contacted them, they were professional journalists, they would have checked it out. This might have been why they rang. Why the hell had he deleted the message without hearing what it had said. He had well and truly shot himself in the foot there. His thoughts were interrupted by the building inspector, who suddenly realised that Charlie was not listening to him. Charlie apologised and they carried on with his full attention.

Janice had decided she had spent enough time at home, and returned to her studio. She decided to follow Leggio's thinking. She wanted to paint her interpretation of how she saw the Mafia, from the original 'men of honour' before world war two, to the horrors of today's killings.

She decided that the first painting should be of Luciano; he had a baby face as a young man. She chose a photo to work on shortly before his arrest in 1974. Well-rounded with trousers and jacket, polo neck sweater and the usual Mafioso sunglasses and his huge cigar. She first made a line drawing, in fact she made several sketches each of which ended up in the rubbish bin. None of them looked like him, then she had a light bulb moment. That was it, they always turned out to be like that, because that's how she should paint him – a distortion of the real man. Once she realised this, it was if someone or some-thing else was driving her hand, the lines flowed. When she had to leave, she had completed the sketch and was so full of a sense of euphoria that she couldn't wait to go home to tell Charlie all about it.

When Charlie came home, he was amazed when he walked in, that the music she played from the kitchen was so far from the Italian he usually encountered; it was a joy to hear.

"Hello, you sound in good spirits."

"Hi Charlie, yes, I had a wonderful day. After breakfast I decided to go back to the studio, I had this wonderful idea, well I actually had it at Luigi's yesterday."

"Great, look, I'm going to take a shower and change, you can tell me everything then." He walked up to her and kissed her on the forehead.

"I'll crack on with tea, roast lamb if it's ok."

"Wonderful," Charlie shouted as he went upstairs. "Wow" he thought to himself, Janice was suddenly like her old self; the fact that she was painting again was a good sign. Then his heart sank. Maybe she was playing, using different tactics, stopped going on about Sicily, to lull him into thinking that she had gone off the idea. Oh well, he would play along, not let her know that he had sussed out her little charade.

For the next two weeks, Janice focused on her painting. Luciano was finished and hung on the wall of her studio. She then focused on her other painting ideas. In the following month or so she had painted quite a few Mafia-related scenes in the same kind of distorted design as Luciano's. She was so proud of them that she used two or three as a window display. She had some negative feedback from the local newspaper's art critic. But that highlighted them, and she sold all three in a few days of each other. Charlie was over the moon to have his wife of old back. She mentioned Leggio a couple of times, but that was usually when the news reported the trial. Other than that, Sicily and the Mafia seemed just a distant memory. Or so he thought.

Eleven

IT WAS AUGUST, good weather, Janice and Charlie were once again happy. But all this would change, anyway for Charlie. He was sure his wife had decided she didn't want to know the truth about her real father anymore. Realising it wouldn't make much difference, he was a criminal in prison for the rest of his life, looking like it. Perhaps she had accepted that it would be too dangerous to pursue. So you can imagine his panic,, deep concern when he came home from the office and found a note on the dining room table.

I'm sorry to let you know like this, but I have gone to Palermo, see you in a week. I thought it was best to do it this way.

"That fucking bitch." He went to the drinks cabinet and poured a large whisky drinking it at once. Then he had another one.

"Stupid woman what the hell have you done?" He sat on the couch and pushed his face into a cushion.

What Janice had done was quite simple; it was while she was in the studio that she decided to call Ansa in Palermo. This way, even if Charlie checked the phone records at home he would have seen that in the last three months, no calls had been made to Italy or Sicily. That's when the idea came to her mind. She could also have her mail re-directed to the studio, so any correspondence she would get wouldn't be known to Charlie. She had been so excited when the letter arrived with her plane tickets. Once they arrived she knew it was really going to happen. Now here she was sitting watching the English country-side flash by as she made her way by coach to Gatwick Airport.

She had decided that she would only spend the afternoon in Naples; she was only away a week so why waste two days looking around the city when she could be on the ferry and in Sicily the next day. She had booked into the airport hotel for the night. Her flight was not until the next morning. It had to be like this, so she could leave the house and Charlie would not know she was going to Sicily. It would be warm in Palermo, so she had packed only a few loose summer dresses, and a suit – she might need to wear that when she entered the prison to see Leggio.

While she was fine dining in the hotel restaurant, Charlie was cooking his tea, which he rarely did. He chuckled at himself, all those times he had griped about the pasta for tea, and what was he having? Pasta! He had a beer and had a TV dinner. He was trying not to worry about Janice, he had to applaud her for her deception, maybe she was Leggio's daughter if she could be so sneaky. Boy he thought he was playing her when all the

100

time she was playing him. He held his can up as if to toast her, then drank from it. He had several more cans before going to bed, he felt that being drunk would be the only way to make sure he went to sleep.

Janice had no such problems, she had a long soak in the bath, then checked again she had not forgotten anything. Before going to bed and drinking a relaxing cup of camomile tea, she turned off the bedside light and went to sleep.

The morning came, she was awake and up bright and early, she made use of the hotel facilities and then went for a continental breakfast, she might as well get used to it, she thought. Doubting that she would get a full English breakfast in Palermo. She checked out and headed to the terminal building, then it was just the long wait until she could go into the checkout lounge. She was getting pretty giddy and thought she'd have a drink to calm her down, then she knew she wouldn't stop at one drink. The last thing she wanted was to get drunk and not be let on the flight. So she settled down with her old favourite a pot of camomile tea. She spoke to a lovely Italian lady, who turned out was an art lover, so the two had a lot to talk about, it passed the time, and soon they both had to go to their respective departure halls.

As Janice was about to board her plane, Charlie sat at his desk trying not to worry. After all, she was an adult, intelligent woman, and no doubt she could take care of herself in a crisis. But that didn't detract from the fact that she was going to confront a notorious gangster, it wouldn't have been so bad if this man had been lower in the pecking order. But Charlie had read about his

101

reputation, some calling him Coccia Di Tacco (bean on fire, or hot head). How would he react when he heard that an English woman claimed to be his daughter, what could that mean for Janice? Would he ignore it, send his foot soldiers to check her out, warn her off, worse? He was portrayed everywhere as a monster. He wiped his hands down his face in sheer despair. Maybe there was only one thing to do? Go to Palermo, at least then he could stand by her side, help protect her, like a husband should his wife. He shook his head, no, that could inflame things, maybe as a single woman, he wouldn't see her as a threat? With a man in tow, he might feel that this was some kind of a ruse. Charlie had heard the news that Leggio had been told by his once proxy Salvatore Riina, who had now assumed to be in command of the Corleonese branch of the Mafia, to keep his mouth shut. Maybe he would think this was a way to make sure he did. There were rumours that for years he feared that harm would come to him, that those who saw him as the thorn in their side, would dispatch him, by some method, get a guard to poison his food. Charlie didn't want to be seen as some kind of hitman. No, it was better he left well alone. The journalists would protect her, he had never thought of that before. She wouldn't be entirely alone, so he should focus on his work, and as Doris Day had sung 'what will be will be'.

It didn't take long to fly from London to Naples. Janice had booked a place by the window, she loved being able to see the clouds as they flew by. The excitement as the plane made its descent and the urban sprawl came into view. Suddenly it hit her, that knot twisted in her stomach and for the first time since she had decided to go to Palermo, the reality of it all dawned on her and she was scared. Before it seemed like a fantasy, she was sure Charlie would find a way to change her mind. Maybe if she hadn't been so deceptive, he might have had a chance. Too late now; she couldn't ask the pilot to turn the plane around so she could get off. No, she was 100% committed now, there was no turning back, that's what she had wanted for almost two years. To know the truth about her parentage. But the sudden awareness that it was not an episode of some Mafia-related drama, she would not be face to face with a fictitious 'Godfather' but with a real Mafia Don Luciano Leggio. Then she consoled herself with the glaringly obvious fact, he might not want to see her. She did as she was wont to do in the event of a crisis, asked the air stewardess for a cup of herbal tea, if they had any.

When they arrived in Naples, she had swung back the other way and was now eager to leave the plane and soak in the Italian air. She wanted to be like the Pope who once got down on his knees and kissed the ground. But she saw it as a melodramatic touch, and anyway if she wanted to do that, shouldn't it be when she reached Sicily her homeland.

Once in the centre she was fascinated by the hustle and bustle of this vibrant city, she regretted now that she decided not to spend a couple of days here. It seemed a real shame to have only a few hours, but she could not change her plans, because she had already agreed on the date and time she would meet in the Ansa office, she could not mess them about.

Before leaving the airport terminal she had bought a map of the city, she would need directions to get to

103

the ferry terminal. She glanced at it now, looking for a restaurant where she could have something to eat. It was so hot, she only had a small suitcase, but she had brought a big coat. Hey, she thought, it could rain in Italy just like it did in the UK. As the scouts would say: 'be prepared'; that was all very well, but having to carry it around in this heat, not a pleasant experience. Feeling slightly light-headed, she stopped at the first available restaurant. Sitting outside under a parasol until a waiter came to her table. She ordered a sandwich and a bottle of sparkling water. She swallowed the water as if she had just crossed the Sahara. When the waiter came back with her sandwich she had drunk it all and asked for a second bottle.

She looked at her watch, it was coming up to 3-00 in the afternoon. She was confused because a clock across the street showed 4-00. Then she realised that she had not altered her watch, someone was watching over her! If she hadn't noticed the error, she would have arrived at the terminal and could have missed the ferry to Palermo. She sat down and looked at people, many tourists, a lot of tourists like her talking, mingling, cameras hung around their necks; like her, they were fascinated by the sights and sounds. Naples was really a beautiful city, but even here the tentacles of the Mafia had reached. The ' Cammora' as it was known here, had done its part in Leggio's plan to kidnap oil tycoon John Paul Getty's grandson for a ransom. This had highlighted the monstrous side of Leggio, when the ransom note was not met. He had cut off part of the boy's ear and sent it with a lock of hair, and had made it clear if the ransom was not met more body parts would be sent. They eventually settled apparently for a smaller demand and the boy was released. She shuddered; was this man really her father? After finishing her water she paid the bill, left a generous tip and went. By now it was cooler, she decided to take the tram to the port. It was a rickety old thing, past its best if the truth be known, but trundled on.

When she saw the ships, the mighty bridge cranes, they took her breath away. It wasn't like a fishing port at home. She had only seen ferries on TV, even then they looked great, but when you saw them seriously, boy, they were huge. She stopped and looked at her map, there were bays for several trips, the one she needed only had departures to and from Palermo, which was good because there was no danger of getting on the wrong ferry. If she didn't get her ticket, she wouldn't be going anywhere. The ferry was supposed to set sail at eight and a quarter, they arrived about nine hours later in Palermo around seven o'clock. She had never sailed on a ship before, and what if she got seasick? Well, it was too late to worry about it now. She had decided not to book a cabin for the night. Would she want to sleep anyway? As a child she had always wanted to be a sailor, her mother said she could always enter the navy when she grew up, she was devastated when Graham told her women did not serve on ships.

"That wasn't good," she had retorted. What was the point of being in the navy if you were stuck on land? She couldn't wait to be on deck as the sunrise broke and she could see Sicily on the horizon, she felt a lump in her throat as she thought about it. Then she jolted herself back to the here and now. It was pretty busy as she sat down. Obviously a lot of people like her had chosen not to have a cabin. Most seemed to be Italian, young men

105

who sat staring at her. The first time since she got off the plane in Naples she felt vulnerable, which increased in intensity when a young man approached where she was sitting.

"Scusi?

"I'm sorry I don't speak Italian," she said nervously, looking behind the young man, at his friends who giggled across the room.

"Italian yes?"

"No no!" she replied, shaking her head. Upon this he turned and returned to his friends, engaged in a conversation, then a different man came across.

"Parla Inglese?"

"Yes, I am Eng... She stopped. "Yes, I speak English."

"I too, I apologise for my friend, he…"

"He only speaks Italian."

"Yes I understood it," she replied rather tersely.

"Are you going to Palermo?"

"I hope so or I'm on the wrong boat."

He screwed up his face, not getting her English humour.

"I'm sorry a joke, haha."

"Oh, I see, are you on vacation?"

Janice was beginning to find the conversation boring and thought in a moment of madness that she knew how she could get rid of him without too much fuss.

"No, I'm going to Palermo for the Maxi trial."

"Because you'd be interested in this, are you a lawyer?"

"Oh no, I suppose you could say I'm on the wrong side of the law. Well, not me personally, but my father."

"Ah, he's a lawyer."

Janice shook her head and prepared to fire the bullet,

which would see this annoyance run for the hills. Or at least she hoped he would. She decided on a subtle approach and would simply drop the name into conversation. He looked like a young intelligent man so she hoped he would make the connection.

"I'm sorry I didn't introduce myself, Gigliola Leggio." She held her hand out. Bingo, the young man's face went ashen, he didn't take her hand to shake but did an about turn and rushed back to his friends; more conversation took place in Italian, before everyone got up and they seemed to leave quickly. Work done. She was only bothered once more, when she had decided to explore the various decks, and had wanted to look at the car deck. A middle-aged man followed her and as she tried to leave he blocked the door, he did not speak English and did not understand what 'no' meant while trying to caress her breasts. So she kept yelling 'Leggio Leggio' and luckily for her a deck steward heard her screams and came to her aid. The man shouted in Italian at the steward waving his arms about. Then he turned and went away. She was the one who was told off for being on the car deck. She was not allowed there while the ship was sailing. She did not know, and apologised profusely, although annoyed that the steward had not asked her if she was all right.

She went and sat on the viewing deck. The ferry accelerated pretty quickly then, as if it was going to cover 167 nautical miles in just under 11 hours and it didn't want to dawdle. In the Mediterranean the sea could be cold, so she had taken the precaution of wearing her coat. Looking at her watch, it would soon be dawn.

She felt rather cold with the wind coming down from the sea, so she decided to go get a hot drink before the sun welcomed a new day, an important day for her. The beginning of a whole new chapter in her life. Let's hope it would not leave her disappointed.

The sunrise was spectacular, but it was nothing compared to the sight of this huge mass appearing on the horizon, the island of Sicily. As they got closer and closer, so it began to take shape. She wondered why their mother had never brought them here as children.

She didn't have to expose her secret; to the locals she would just be another tourist on holiday with her family. Had she not wanted to see her parents, did they really consider she was dead to them? Janice had been so pre-occupied with this train of thought, she had quite a shock when she looked up. There in the distance she could just make out the huge port cranes like the ones that she had marvelled at in Naples. There before her eyes was Palermo. She started getting excited, she had no idea why she started crying, she'd never been here before. Then after reading and seeing so many photos not only of Palermo, but of the island as a whole, she felt as if she had finally come home.

It didn't take long before she was joined by crowds of other passengers who each wanted to get their own vantage point to enjoy the thrill of arriving at port. In fact it just looked like a mirror image of the port of Naples. Except the background buildings were very different. Once docked, she disembarked with her fellow passengers and headed to a taxi rank. She had planned to stay not in Palermo but in Cefalu, in English terms what would be seen as a seaside resort. It was only when they got some way from the city that she began to realise that it was not as close to Palermo as she thought. It was actually some distance away the taxi driver told her. So she ordered him to turn around, and take her back to Palermo, where she would find a hotel.

Janice recalled that when she left the ferry and walked to the taxi rank she had noticed a large hotel right in front of the port entrance across the street. She'd try there. She was lucky, they had a single room, she was shown up to it and immediately rang room service for tea and some unbuttered toast. She looked out of the window of her room and saw a great view of the sea, with some smaller cranes in the foreground. It was only 8-30, she was shattered and decided after her light breakfast that she would take a quick bath and then have a sleep. She wasn't due to be at the press office till tomorrow, so there was no rush.

Her order was delivered, it was nice to be able to make her own tea, so she could have it as she liked. She had brought some Dairylea from home because she wasn't sure how she would deal with the food and couldn't live on pasta for a week. She spread some of this on her toast and sunk into the armchair while savouring her tea. It was already so hot, but it was a different kind of heat from what they had at home. She had never been to such a hot place, except maybe the local sauna, but would that count? She felt stupid when she had to go looking for a maid to ask how the bathroom taps turned on. She had tried to turn both left and right, but no water came out. The only thing she hadn't tried was to lift the tap handle up. She thanked the maid and gave her a tip for taking time to come and show her. It was too hot for a normal type of bath that she would have if she were at home. So it was just lukewarm, she felt sure she would spend most of the day sitting in the water, it was the only place she felt really cool. The only reason she left the bath was the need to sleep. It was surreal as she slipped between the cool cotton sheets, it wasn't long before she drifted away to sleep.

Twelve

WHEN SHE EVENTUALLY woke up it was well after three. She ordered room service and slipped on a pale blue dress. After her latest cup of tea, she decided it was time to hit the streets. Her first visit would be to see the prison. It was within walking distance of the hotel. Now it was the middle of the afternoon it was not as warm so it would be a pleasant stroll.

You could not escape its presence, high steel mesh fencing seemed to extend down the road for miles. There were heavily armed policemen, soldiers in armoured cars; this, you could tell, was no ordinary prison. She continued to walk along the perimeter on the footpath on the opposite side of the road. There was a small sea wall, she sat on that near what she assumed was the main gate. Taking out her camera she started to take some photographs. Not a good idea it turned out. Before she knew it this big burly soldier with a massive gun walked across the road and began to rant in Italian, then pointed at her camera.

She shrugged her shoulders, just kept repeating 'Non Capire' that she did not understand.

He snatched her camera, pointed his finger at it and said 'no'.

It was then she realised he was telling her she must not take photographs. She nodded she understood, and put her camera away, sitting back down on the small wall. He again started to rant at her, pushing her up off the wall, and waving his hand, gestured she should leave. With a gun like he was holding she did not need to be told twice, and hastily walked back the way she had come.

She had taken a complimentary map from the hotel lobby so looking at that she decided to go into the city, at least she would be free to take photographs there. The map was not much help; she had never been good with maps, recalling her days in the Girl Guides, smiling to herself; whenever she was required to use a map, she inevitably got lost. She shoved the map in her shoulder bag and just followed what looked like a main road. She seemed to go around the houses but eventually hit the city centre. Even though it was Sunday it was still busy, with tourists like her eager to see the treasure this vibrant city had. She was captivated by the numerous carved statues, the work of master stonemasons. It was breath-taking. She looked around for somewhere so she could sit in some shade and have a cool drink out of the sun. There was a beautiful area of grass with benches and an ornate water fountain, to the side was a street food seller, maybe he would have a drink, she wondered what the food might be, she was starting to feel hunger pangs but being a fussy eater, he might not have anything she would eat on offer. She was in luck, he was a seafood seller, so with a box of mussels, cockles and prawns which she would die for, she went and sat on a bench two sachets of malt vinegar in hand to garnish her food with. It was then that she noticed them. To start with she thought she was just letting her imagination run away with her. Would anyone especially at this particular time with the Maxi trial going on, really want to bring attention to themselves by looking like two extras from the 'Godfather'? They could be a couple of over zealous movie buffs, both men wore dark suits, one had a bright white shirt on, the slightly tall one had a black shirt, he looked like an undertaker, she laughed to herself, if they were Mafioso was that his nick name? Both had mirrored shades, they were perfect stereotypical Mafioso types.

Janice told herself to get a grip, lots of people if she looked around would be dressed just the same. But as she scanned her eyes around where she sat, yes there were lots of people with various designs of sun glasses, but no one else seemed to be in a suit. She calmed herself by realising she would be a little jumpy to start with, but no one else knew, apart from the journalists, why she was here. So she should finish her prawns, then take a leisurely stroll down to the sea front and chill out. There seemed little chance of that, because after she discarded her rubbish in a nearby bin, she noticed the two men had got up, they were watching her, not only that but as she left, they started to follow discreetly behind her. She was unsure what to do. The best thing would be to go back to her hotel, yes they would know where she was staying, but in the confines of that she would at least be safe. Maybe she should mention it to the hotel management, then if they were still outside, hotel security could have a word in their ear. Then she would have to explain the whole business with Leggio; no, she would deal with it in her own way.

Once back at the hotel she looked carefully from behind her curtains; they were both at the other side of the road talking to some other men, so they were too busy to notice she might be looking at them. She felt that cold shiver up her spine; one of the men talking to them was Fabio, the hotel waiter. She pulled away from the window and went to the mini bar, taking out a small whisky miniature she didn't bother with a glass and just swigged it from the bottle. Of course it made her cough as it slid down her gullet, but she had needed that drink. She never left her room again that day, fearful that there was some kind of conspiracy going on, to maybe not harm her in some way, but to find out what her game was. Fabio could be the inside mole. God, Charlie had been right, it was foolish of her to come here, it was only the first day here and she was already shitting herself. She decided she would see the journalists in the morning, see if Leggio would see her. If it was not going to go anywhere, then she would change her flight and get the hell out of here while she still had the ability to breathe in the Sicilian air!

When she awoke, it was another beautiful day, she had missed breakfast but was not too bothered she didn't feel as if she would keep any food down at the moment. She rang room service for some tea, and then started to get organised. She checked all her documents, yet again that knot appeared in her stomach twisting ever tighter. The realisation that it was really happening, today she would set the train in motion and there would be no way to stop it unless she purposely derailed it. But why would she want to do that? Was this not what she had wanted, but did she want her face on the front of every newspaper, not just in Italy but the world over? Her tea arrived so she had to leave the soul searching. She sipped her tea and peeped out behind the curtain, yes there they were, Yin and Yang as she had named her two mysterious bodyguards, across the street having a crafty cigarette, she had not seen them smoking before. They would see her as soon as she left the hotel. Rather than be worried about them, she felt she should embrace their presence. It gave her a strange sense of security, someone some-where was taking her seriously, she decided to embrace this new found fame, with Yin and Yang she was invin-cible. She was getting dressed when she had the thought, she assumed these two men were Mafioso, but they could easily be plain clothes policemen, then would they wear suits, they did stand out, maybe that was the point. So those who might want to harm her knew the police were watching her. She decided to wear a short sleeved blouse that had a thin velvet bow around the neck, and a cream linen skirt. She looked in the full length mirror. My God, she looked so English, she thought. But the reporters would not care what she was wearing, she was not taking part in a fashion show. She checked her documents once again and decided to set off early. She had no idea where she was going. Fabio had drawn her a crude map, she had to head for a road called Via Emerico Amari; she suggested to him it might be better to get a taxi but he shook his head, traffic was a nightmare in the city, walking would be far quicker. She laughed to herself, she could always ask Yin and Yang to show her the way; instead of them following her, she could follow them! She took her camera with her, it would be nice to have another wander around after the meeting, take some photographs to show Charlie, then would he be interested? As she left the hotel, she waved at the two men, who as expected did not respond, except to cross the road to accompany her a few paces behind.

She got lost a couple of times but with the help of a Carabinieri, who drew her a new map, she eventually arrived at Number 8, the offices of Ansa, not as early as she would have liked. It was another hot day, Fabio had told her to drink plenty of water, and to stay in the shade as much as possible, until her body adapted to the change in climate. Within a couple of days she would be more comfortable with the heat. She hoped so, at the moment she was craving that lukewarm bath again. She had never been a hot weather person, snow and ice was more her thing. Janice took another long drink of water. Discarded the bottle in a near by bin, took a deep breath in and walked into the reception. She was sweating profusely shaking at the same time. This was it, momentarily she thought she should turn and leave, but that was not going to happen now as a tall bearded man approached her.

"Buongiorno, Signorita Richards. Please come this way, I am Saverio Mazzoto, forgive me for not addressing you as Miss Leggio, but we have to be careful."

"Oh not at all, I understand until you have seen my documents I could be anyone."

"Si come this way and meet my colleague Giuseppe." He gestured that she should follow him upstairs to an office; there were lots of desks, people on telephones chattering away, others on typewriters, a typical news office she thought as she was guided to a desk at the far end near the window. Giuseppe shook her hand, and then once seated she told them why she believed she was an illegitimate daughter of the one of the world's most notorious Mafia 'Godfathers' Luciano Leggio.

Janice took out her small leather document holder and removed the various items within it. Both reporters looked at each document in turn scribbling notes in short hand, occasionally chatting in Italian to each other, something she thought was terribly rude.

"Eh Dom come and take these and photocopy them," Saverio shouted across the office.

"Well we did not realise your mother came from Sicily."

"I didn't know either until after she died, it was by sheer chance I found my birth certificate. In England a lot of people like to trace their family tree. I always wondered why I could never find relatives on my mother's side."

"She never talked about Sicily?"

"Oh good God no, these letters they shed light on the whole sorry mess. I believe some of the content is in Sicilian dialect." She passed the letters across.

"We have spoken with Leggio, he seemed to think you were mistaken, but these letters, documents from the Italian authorities, do suggest there could be some truth to it. Then again we have to bear in mind she might have just said it was Leggio. Without your mother's testimony it's all a bit up in the air. Because of the Maxi trial, security has to be of paramount importance, so the prison authorities have refused permission for us to take you to see Leggio, but in view of this evidence, we will send this across to the prison governor and see if he might change his mind. In the meantime we would like to take you to Corleone, the Mayor of the town is keen to meet you, and there is the possibility that some of Leggio's family might also want to cast an eye over you."

Janice sat frozen to the chair, they wanted to take her to Leggio's home turf, would that be wise? Yin and Yang could not protect her there. But isn't this what she had wanted?

"Gigliola, would you like that? You don't mind me calling you that, or would you prefer Janice?" Saverio asked; he was obviously the senior reporter, as Giuseppe hardly said much at all. In fact she thought he looked quite scared.

"No Gigliola is fine; it is after all my birth name, it is time I stopped my mother's charade and was allowed to be myself. To go to Corleone would be wonderful, who knows if there might be some of my mother's relations. It could be a whole new chapter."

"Good, tomorrow after lunch, would that fit with your plans?"

"Oh I am free whenever you need me to be."

"Good good, we will meet here tomorrow then about 1-30. Is there anything else we can help you with?"

"There is one thing, this is going to sound crazy, but there are two men following me. I first noticed them yesterday afternoon, I went for a walk into the city centre that's when I noticed them, they then followed me back to my hotel, and again today they followed me here."

"Have you told the police?"

"No I thought that they would think I was some strange English woman with an over-active imagination."

"The police are aware you are on the island, we were duty bound to inform them. So they know all about you."

"Oh I see, there was I thinking I could just fade into the background."

"That, if you don't mind me saying, is a touch naive. If this turns out to be true, your life will be very different, you may have to follow your mother's lead and change your identity."

"Really, is it that serious?"

"My dear young lady, I do hope for your sake this is not just some kind of English folly, you do not mess with the Mafia, many people in this city, on this Island would be all too quick to remind you of this."

Janice felt a lump in her throat, she had come with honest intentions, she was not playing a game, she had evidence. If they took it seriously then that was the problem Yin and Yang were proof someone else was also taking it seriously. She must have looked faint, because the older journalist asked her if she was ok? She said she was fine.

The two journalists stood up and each shook her hand.

"Until tomorrow then."

As Janice exited the office they watched her through the window and saw for themselves the two men.

"Yes she is right, she is being followed; we had better check with the prison; if it's not Leggio's men, we might need to tell the police, she could be in danger."

"Do you think it is wise to take her to Corleone then?"

"I don't know Giuseppe, but we have to follow the

story. I mean why would a young woman from the UK come all this way to prove a man who we know is a psychopathic monster, is her biological father? Not only that but her documents seem to point to it being the truth."

Gigliola suddenly felt hungry, there were no shortage of traders selling street food, but none of it appealed to her.

So she wandered around, eventually finding a bakery, where she bought some freshly baked bread rolls. Not far down from the bakery she spotted a delicatessen and so with bread and ham in hand she found a shaded bench where she sat down to think about the day's events. She was sad that she had been so close to meeting Luciano, but the damned Maxi trial had got in the way. Maybe the governor would change his mind once he had seen the documents. But there were things to be cheerful about, tomorrow she was going to Corleone, meeting the mayor having photographs taken with him and other council members. Suddenly she felt like she really belonged here. She glanced around to see if her companions Yin and Yang were about, or had got fed up and had scampered off. But no, she eventually spotted them eating an ice cream in the shade of a beautiful tree. She smiled to herself, what an image: two Mafioso eating ice cream, how uncool was that? She decided to take a photograph of them, but that did not go down too well, they both turned away. Silly really she thought, with their mirrored shades they would not be recognisable.

Having satisfied her appetite she made her way

back to the sea front, she loved the Marina and she had always wanted a yacht; there were big ones, little ones, even ocean-going ones. It was relaxing sitting on a bench looking out to sea, the sun shining, a cool breeze blowing in, so she was not too hot. She so wished Charlie was here, then he could have gone with her to Corleone. Corleone. She was really going there tomorrow; she recalled the painting Leggio had done of the town, she would see for herself if he had captured the town as it really was.

She knew herself as a fellow artist how hard it could be sometimes trying to paint something from memory. Her thoughts were interrupted by a shadow standing over her. She looked up and saw a tall Moroccan-looking man.

"Scusi," he said gesturing if he may sit beside her. Suddenly Yin and Yang seemed to appear from nowhere; she looked directly at them and shook her head. They seemed to understand what she was gesturing and withdrew.

"No Italiano," she said as he sat down.

"Oh that's ok I speak English, you are English?"

"No, Sicilian," she replied, after all she was being truthful as far as she knew at present. The man screwed his face up not understanding.

"Sicilian and you do not speak Italian, that's quite odd."

"I grew up in England, my parents are Sicilian."

"I understand now, have you come back home with your parents to live?"

Gigliola was getting annoyed again, why did these men home in on her, she just wanted to sit in the sun and enjoy the view without the third degree.

"My mother's dead, my father is in prison, and before you ask, yes here in the Ucciardone down the road."

"I am sorry to hear that. Has he been in prison long?"

"Since 1974, he is a Mafioso."

"Mafioso, ah well everyone in Palermo is one of those," he said quite flippantly.

"So are you one, you might know my father, Luciano Leggio. Oh then you might be on the other side?"

"Luciano Leggio?"

"Yes, is that a problem for you?" She decided to have a little bit of fun at the expense of this guy, he was a touch too smarmy for her liking.

"Those two men, they are my bodyguards, she leant in towards him, they go everywhere with me, I can not go to the bathroom without them standing outside."

"Maybe I could help you?"

"Oh and how would you do that?" she enquired.

"I could be your bodyguard, show you around the island."

She wondered if this sudden desire to help her had anything to do with the fact she had just told him who her father was, or was he more concerned with getting his hands down her pants; she shuddered when she thought about that.

"Oh that's very good of you to offer, but I should stick with my present bodyguards, after all my father might be angry otherwise; even though I am his daughter, I would not like to cross him. But thank you anyway." Gigliola got up and started to walk away from the young man.

"If you're sure," he called after her; she gave no response and waited to cross the road. There was a wine bar and she felt like a cool glass of Sicilian wine. She glanced over her shoulder and saw the two men walking a short distance behind, slowing down so they did not catch up with her before, she had crossed the road. Once in the wine bar, she watched in the mirror that covered the back wall behind the bar; these two men were definitely shadowing her, as she saw them enter and close the door. They stood to one side of it, a few of the customers had looked up at them when they had first entered, then gone back to their conversations unfazed by their arrival. She ordered a large white wine and sat down on a stool at the bar. That way she could keep an eye on what was going on behind her.

She was starting to relax listening to the pleasant background music when her idyll was shattered by the arrival of a middle-aged man who started to hassle her. He did not speak a word of English and did seem more than a little tipsy. Even the barman told him to behave and not to hassle the customers. But he seemed not to listen. Gigliola froze when she noticed one of her shadows walking up towards the bar, he whispered something in the man's ear and they both went outside. The barman who spoke excellent English apologised for the customer's outrageous behaviour, and went on to say he was not far from being barred. He had a habit of coming on to tourists. She said it was no problem. They had the same kind of situation in the UK, especially when guys were drunk. Their conversation was interrupted by the return of her hassler; he approached her very sheepishly and said something to her in Italian. The barman said he was apologising, and to show no hard feelings he would like to buy her a drink. She declined the offer, drank the last of her wine and got up to leave; as she approached the door, the taller bodyguard she called Yang opened the door for her, they exchanged a brief look, but it said so much to her. He gestured she should leave first. She thanked them for their help, but neither spoke, maybe they did not speak English? They stayed some distance behind as she walked back to the hotel; just before she went in, she turned as if she was going to wave goodbye, but they had both vanished as quickly as they had previously appeared. She could not get that look out of her mind, it was as if he had tried to communicate with her by using his eyes in some cryptic way. She could not help but wonder if there was some sexual context behind it. Unbeknown to her she would soon have her answer.

It was still quite early, so she went into the hotel bar, had a large whisky, and then went up to her room. It was strange that there was a knock on her door, she opened it and could not believe who was standing there. It was Yang.

"Gigliola, can I come in?" He never waited for her reply, just walked in and closed the door.

"Excuse me you cannot just invite yourself into my room like this. Who are you? How do you know my name? Why are you here, why are you following me, are you one of Leggio's men?" She did not look at him, just stared towards the window. What was going to happen, was he going to harm her? She was terrified.

"So many questions, none of which with the exception of one I can answer."

"So which one can you answer?" she turned and looked directly at him.

"I wanted to meet you. After our brief look when you were leaving the wine bar, I so wanted to talk to you." He took of his shades and revealed his brown almost dark chocolate coloured eyes.

"Why, because I am English. Only it seems I am in fact Sicilian."

"Does that bother you?" He seemed very edgy.

"No, it's the father that bothers me."

"Gigliola, can I kiss you? God I want you. I should not be here really, but it's been killing me ever since we first started shadowing you."

"God what an ego you must have, expect me to fall at your feet. I might not want you." She tried to hide the fact she felt the same.

He gave a little laugh. "Oh no Gigliola, when we exchanged that brief look, then just now, I read your body language when I took my shades off, you want it too, I know you do."

"Very vain aren't you, just because you're so hand-some and sexy."

"Thank you, so you must find me pleasing to the eye."

"Bet you look even sexier naked," she said almost whispering.

He walked up to her, leant forward and kissed her so gently; once he was sure she would be responsive he wrapped his arms around her and kissed her with such passion. She could feel he was becoming aroused. Where would this end? With them both naked in bed. But suddenly he pulled away, and swore to himself.

"No, this is wrong, I am putting you in danger. I must not let my own selfish desires put you in an impossible situation." He looked agitated, cross with himself.

"No one knows you are here do they?" she asked trying to reassure him.

"No. Fabio let me in via the fire exit, so my colleague did not see me coming into the hotel. I just had to see you."

"Then there is no problem." She went up to him and tried to caress him.

"No, I should never have come, what the hell was I thinking? Letting lust get the better of me."

"You come in here to my room, tease me, kiss me, start feelings of desire within me, then think you can just switch off. Please make love to me, let me feel you inside of me, a happy memory to take home to England."

"No, no I must fight this. I am so sorry. I should go. It was stupid of me to come in the first place."

"You bastard." She slapped his face, but he just took her in his arms and kissed her again.

"Oh that's another question answered. Like violence, turn you on does it, should I slap you again, Mr Mafioso? Might you give in then?"

"Gigliola, what have you done to me. I do not normally display such a loss of self control."

"Can I help it if you find me sexually pleasing? Give in to it, let the feelings out. Let's share a few hours of passion together. I promise on my life I will tell no one. Leggio will not know about it."

"No, I must go." He tried to go to the door. "Please Gigliola, don't make this harder than it already is. Please let me go before it's too late."

She slipped her dress off and removed her bra. He momentarily lost control and kissed and caressed her breasts, before he regained his composure, manhandled her out of the way, opened the door and left. She was devastated, and took to drink. She decided to ring home.

"Hi Charlie," she said with a slurred voice; there was no response, just the sound of a dead line.

"Haha, he hung up Luciano, I think that means he is still cross, oops.

Thirteen

GIGLIOLA ARRIVED AT the Ansa office in good time. She was dressed in a pale blue chiffon dress and wearing a solid gold crucifix, with a small clutch bag. She decided against taking her camera, any photographs she could get copies of from the journalist. There was just Saverio, and a photographer. She was reminded of her first car journey in Sicily as they drove on the highway, it was like the motorway back in the UK. She felt nervous, which wasn't helped by the driving skills of Saverio who drove like a maniac. There was not much conversation; when it did occur it was between her two companions and in Italian. So she gazed out of the window; once they left the suburbs of Palermo the scenery was just stunning; soon they were off the highway onto the rural roads. They drove up towards a mountain range. Saverio explained that Corleone was in a basin, some of the town was built onto the mountain side, not far from the town was a beautiful nature reserve, with its own waterfall. It took about an hour to reach the town.

As they drove up a narrow street, Gigliola noticed bunting hanging from the olde worlde houses; some looked derelict, unloved, others brightly coloured like the ones in Leggio's painting he had sent to her. As they drove into the town square there were people everywhere, some would be tourists; after all, since the 'Godfather' Corleone had become a mecca for aficionados of the film. So it brought visitors and their money into the town. Others she had no doubt had come to look at the woman who claimed to be the daughter of one of their notorious sons.

As the car pulled up she saw all these men lined up obviously waiting to greet her. She felt sick, her heart was pounding, she was sure that as soon as she stepped from the car she would faint. She took deep breaths as Saverio opened the car door for her to exit. The mayor rushed up and hugged her, then shaking her hand frantically, chattering away in Italian, then it could have been the Sicilian dialect. Any previous nervousness vanished, as one after another shook her hand and called her signorina Leggio, kissing her cheeks. She was totally sucked in by it all.

There were numerous photographs two way conversations as, questions were asked in Italian, then translated in to English for her reply, then back into Italian. People cheered, complete strangers came to shake her hand. Then time seemed to stand still, the mayor took her by the arm and led her to an elderly lady, she had black curly hair that sat just above her shoulders. She wore a jacket with an ornate brooch on the lapel. She was introduced as Maria-Antonina, Luciano Leggio's sister. She muttered something, she did not hug Gigliola but did take her hand briefly. She gazed at her as if she was looking for any resemblance, that would prove that the English lady was who she claimed to be. Maybe Leggio had asked her to be there; he trusted his sister, that was obvious because why else would he have entrusted her with his estate to run in his absence. If Maria-Antonina believed she was his daughter, would he accept her word, and welcome Gigliola into the bosom of his family?

His sister turned and slowly walked away, nothing else was said. That was it, it was all over, life went back to normal, those that had come into the square just to gawk at her went back to their houses, the mayor and his colleagues went back to their offices, and apart from a few people milling about, they stood alone in the car-park. Was this her five minutes of fame, the Godfather's daughter meeting the people of the town he had terrorised for years? Dragged it down into the gutter. Yet as she sat in the car back to Palermo, she thought of all those who had cheered, had wanted to shake her hand, they did not see the horrors he had committed, to them he was their hero. Her's he was not; they might share blood, but that was all. Suddenly she had come to realise, she did not care if he did not want to meet with her. She did not want to look into those murderous eyes, at last she had finally accepted the reality of it all, and she did not like what she saw. Coming to Sicily to see him had been a mistake. But that was a decision she would have to live with, what was done was done. The clock could not be turned back, the can of worms remained open, she was just going to have to do the classic English thing and 'bite the bullet and get on with it'.

When they got back to the office, it was all left very

much in the air. She didn't ask what happened next, just got out of the car, said thank you, shook their hands and went. Not far from the hotel going up towards the Marina was a small side road, where a catering van was parked; it had a few tables and chairs opposite. She had stopped there the day before and had a cool drink and some crisps. She did the same today. There was so much to think about, if it was in the paper tomorrow, what would it mean for her? At the moment only a handful of people knew she was not just another tourist, Tomorrow she might wake up and the whole world would know who she was.

God if it was in the British press, what would her friends make of it, and Charlie, oh God Charlie how would he deal with it. Was divorce on the horizon? She was just getting up to leave, when the Moroccan guy she had met earlier noticed her as he was walking by.

"Hello again," he shouted as he walked towards her.

"So we meet again?" She was not pleased to see him, she could make a scene and Yin and Yang might come and have a word with him, like they did with the guy in the wine-bar. But she had not seen them since she had returned from Corleone.

"Oh please say you will let me show you some of the island. I can outwit your bodyguards then you can have some fun. Without them watching your every move."

"That's so sweet, but really I can show myself around."

"There are some men who will try it on with you, I will just be a friend, I would not want to upset your father." What she did not know was, this guy had been asking questions about her, he had plans for this naive English woman.

132

"Ok, for today, we will visit the sea front, maybe there is a beach?"

"Great, tell me your name? I am Ahmed."

"Gigliola."

"Erm a good Italian name. So we go to the seafront yes?"

"Yes, but I will need to go to the hotel first for my swimming costume and towel."

"Where are you staying?" He already knew that, but he could not let her know.

"The President, just down the road, opposite the port."

"Yes, I know it, I pass it everyday on my way to work."

"Oh what do you do?"

"I am a fisherman."

"I am so envious, I love the sea, I always wanted to be a sailor."

"I have an idea, why do we not go and see my boss, he might take you out for a short trip."

She agreed as it was in the same direction as the hotel, it sounded like a great idea. Maybe this guy was not so bad after all. She never got her boat trip, Ahmed's boss was not there when they arrived, they never got to the beach either. In fact the whole afternoon was somewhat of a disappointment. It ended in anger, when Ahmed thinking it would be a laugh, took her up on a Ferris wheel and had it stopped at the top. She was terrified as the chair swung in the wind, by the time she was back on the ground she was close to tears. She stormed off back to the hotel.

She was just getting dressed when her phone rang, there was a gentleman with some flowers in reception.

She told them she would be down shortly. When she eventually got to reception she was not surprised to see Ahmed. He apologised profusely and asked if he could make it up to her. He had asked his boss about the boat trip and he had agreed. But it would have to be this morning. She was unsure at first, but it could be fun and it would be nice to see the island from the sea in a little boat; maybe they could sail along the coast? So she agreed, she took the flowers to her room and Maria the maid got her a vase. Then, small handbag over her shoulder, she went down to go with Ahmed.

They chatted as they walked along to the part of the port where the fishing boats were moored. Disappointment fell down her face when she saw this small boat, not much bigger than the rowing boats back home on her local river. Did this rickety old thing go to sea?

"Hamaz, this is the lady I told you about." Ahmed almost pulled her towards his boss. He approached her, pushed her hair away to one side then stroked his hand down her cheek.

"Beautiful English Rose yes"

"No Sicilian," she replied feeling more than a little uncomfortable.

"Hamaz, she says she is Leggio's daughter."

"Leggio, Leggio…" He started to laugh, then Ahmed also started to laugh.

"Let me tell you something my so called Mafia Princess, Leggio is a joke now in Sicily. Oh yes, once he was a big boss, not anymore; he is a stupid old man, who has nothing left to do but paint. Some say he can't paint a daisy, that other people do the painting and he just adds his name. You think those two men are his, your so-called bodyguards; how do you know I have not paid them to follow you?" That smarmy tone was evident in Ahmed's voice once again. She suddenly realised he had a point.

"So did you, shall we go ask them?"It was obvious to her that he had tried to pull the wool over her eyes, his reaction giving him away, that he had lied. She tried to understand what this man wanted from her, he bought her flowers then treated her with contempt.

"So the boat trip," Ahmed said changing the subject, she was not so sure she wanted to go to sea in that excuse for a boat. When Ahmed had said his boss had a fishing boat, she thought he meant one like she had seen at Whitby, a proper trawler type boat.

"He does not want money, for the trip, he wants sex." Ahmed said quietly.

"What, no, no way, I am no prostitute, how dare you suggest such a thing." She decided against making a scene, instead she simply said she had gone off the idea of going to sea and promptly walked off. Leaving Ahmed to explain to his boss that she had not previously known that was the deal.

There was no sign of her Guardian Angels she felt vulnerable, unsure what she should do. Where were they, had they been called off? She had not heard from the journalists, had Leggio seen the evidence and had discredited it. Was she now on her own? She had trusted Ahmed, thought he was a friend, but he had turned out to be a snake in the grass, bloody flowers they would go in the bin when she got back to the hotel.

Ahmed realised he had upset her again, so rushed to the hotel, he was relieved there were no sign of her

135

bodyguards, or he could be on his knees begging forgiveness. When he got there he asked the receptionist to ring her room, but she refused to see him. He was not one to be daunted so went into the bar, got himself a drink and casually brought her into conversation. He said he wanted to send a bottle of wine to her room, but had forgotten the room number. Fabio overheard and without stopping to think said what the number was. Ahmed finished his drink and started to leave the bar.

"Sir, don't forget the wine," the barman shouted after him, but Ahmed just went.

Gigliola was not pleased to see him when she opened the door, and tried to shut it but Ahmed was too strong and pushed his way in.

"Look I am sorry, really I did not know my boss wanted..."

"Save it, what is your game, you insult me, you insult my father, I don't like silly games."

"I know I like you, I like you a lot, not because of who your father is, you're not only beautiful but interesting – what's the word? Ah yes, sophisticated, I mean you no disrespect. Please let me take you to a wonderful trattoria I know, where you can taste true Sicilian food, that will leave you wanting more."

"I do not like Sicilian food, I have a simple palette." She went and looked out of the window to see if Yin and Yang were there. They could be but were not openly visible to her.

"Please Gigliola, give me one more chance." He got on his knees and held his hands as if in prayer.

"For God's sake get up. Sea food."

"I am sorry, sea food?"

"That's what I like to eat."

"You mean we will go out to eat?"

"I must be mad, but I can't stand this charade anymore."

"You will not be disappointed, my friend she has a cafe, she is an excellent cook, she will cook just for us. Yes?"

She should have known better, one minute he was taking her to a fancy trattoria, then suddenly it's his friend's cafe. She just did not have the energy to argue, it was too hot, she was exhausted, and he would just plague her if she continued to refuse. He was becoming an irritation she could really do without.

Then she had Yin and Yang, they would be shadowing her, so what could go wrong? Ahmed said he would return to the hotel at 6-30, the cafe closed at 6 it was on a side street, so did not get tourist custom. He was sure Adelina would cook for them. She would sit down to a feast of sea food. He went and left Gigliola to do her own thing.

She decided she was not going to any special effort, after all this was not a date, she saw it as a way to get rid of this man, he clung to her like a leech, she just wanted rid of him, but would let him down gently to avoid any unpleasantness. She waited in the lobby for him. She had decided to look like a prim and proper English woman, nothing fancy, that way she would look more matronly and might defuse any sexual desire he might have for her.

Arriving on time he obviously thought it was a date, he had a shirt on, no tie, and neatly pressed camel coloured slacks. His thick black hair combed back and covered in some kind of hair product to keep it in place. She wanted to laugh because he looked as if he had stuck his head in the chip pan. He kissed her cheek and noticed how she flinched. But never said anything. He led her outside and off they went.

She tried to glance behind without making it seem obvious to him, but he was ahead of her.

"Yes, they are following us, did you think they wouldn't?"

"I thought they might have a night off, they must have to eat." She said trying to make it seem she was annoyed they were there.

They walked up the road that went around the shoreline to the Marina, but turned off to the right up a side road. This looked like the slum area of Palermo, where the poor lived, the down and outs the drug takers. The houses, if she could call them that, were in effect derelict buildings, broken windows, some roofless so they looked like a box made from bricks.

"A lot of these buildings are like this because of your fathers lot!"Ahmed seemed angry about it.

"Why do you say that?"

"Property, corrupt politicians on the make, selling contracts to the Mafia, they were going to do big things, well they said they were, but as you can see, there are just slums."

"I am sorry, but what can I do?"

"Have a word with him."

It was then that she realised Ahmed really thought she had Leggio's ear. How would he react if he found out the two had never met? That she had no idea who the two men were. She had to make sure he didn't find out or she could be in real danger.

They walked along further slum like streets, then arrived at their destination. A small cafe, there were a few tables inside and a high counter to the rear. As soon as Ahmed entered an elderly lady rushed from the kitchen and came up to her hugging and kissing her, chattering away in Italian. For some reason she seemed to think she was Ahmed's wife. Gesturing they both sit down she then disappeared into the kitchen and returned with a large carafe of wine. She poured two glasses but Ahmed refused his and said he would have water instead.

He had been true to his word and Adelina was indeed a good cook; then, there was not a lot to do with sea food. The fried squid was quite palatable, she had never had that before, and there were huge prawns that she really enjoyed. Ahmed excused himself saying he wanted to have a cigarette. That had been his excuse to see if her men were about. They were loitering down the road leaning against a small wall. They looked up at him, but stayed where they were. He finished his cigarette and told Adelina she could lock the front door, they would leave via the kitchen, she could go and he would put the latch on when they left. Gigliola said she was full and felt a little sleepy. In fact if truth be known she appeared to be tipsy. Ahmed helped her get up from the chair, and took her through the kitchen and out of the back door, making sure it was locked. They turned to the right and he helped her go up a stone staircase. She did not really know what was going on, but just leaned against Ahmed. Eventually they went through a door, and he sat her down in a wicker peacock chair.

"What is she doing here?" she heard an angry voice say; she could make out a faint image of another man.

"She is staying tonight, you have a problem with that?" Ahmed asked.

"But she is a woman, we cannot have her here."

"Shut up this is my house, I say who stays here not you, unless you want to find somewhere else to live? No, I thought not. Now leave us."

"Come Gigliola you need to sleep." He led her into another room, it had no door, just a curtain to afford privacy. He just pushed her down, so she fell on to a mattress on the floor. He stripped to his boxer shorts and lay down beside her. She groaned a bit, totally out of it. He unfastened her blouse and undid her front opening bra and started squeezing her breasts, before he sucked hard on her nipple like a baby suckling for milk, he then bit them. Gigliola offered little resistance but when he slid her pants down and started to lay on top of her and he was just going to penetrate her, that she started to realise what was happening; something stirred in her, she screamed and struggled to get off the mattress. Managing to get up off the floor, semi-naked she fled from the room, almost getting tangled in the curtain. She stumbled towards a table, feeling in the dark for anything she could use to defend herself; when she felt the blade of a knife, she took it in her hand. By now the whole house was awake and the light had been turned on.

The other men looked in horror at this half-dressed woman, her hair dishevelled, the terror etched on her face, as she swung the knife frantically from left to right screaming in English she would stab anyone who got too close.

"Ahmed what have you done?" an older man screamed at him.

"She wanted it, she let me kiss her fucking tits, she teased me."

"No, look at her, she does not look to me like she wanted it. How many times Ahmed, how many times are you going to do this? You're an animal, you should respect a woman, not treat them like this."

Ahmed just shrugged his shoulders and said he was going back to bed; he had work in the morning.

The others did likewise, except for the man who had told Ahmed off; he tried to calm Gigliola but she was in no mood to calm down. She sat in the peacock chair, the knife firmly grasped in both hands. In the end the man decided it was best he left her alone, and returned to his own bed. She dare not close her eyes, she feared for her life, it was soon dawn and Ahmed got up to go to work.

"You fucking bitch," he said as he got a drink of water.

"You raped me, you took advantage of me."

"You came for the meal, I did not force you."

"You told Adelina I was your wife."

"No, she assumed you were. You could have told her you weren't."

"Oh yes when she speaks no English and I speak very little Italian, yes that would have worked. You drugged me didn't you, put something in the wine, is that why you didn't drink any? When my father hears about this."

"Your father, what is he going to do? Tell the police? Or are you going to go see if your two bodyguards are out there. Daddy will not be pleased with them will he. They saw you come here of your own free will. I haven't time for this, I have to go to work. I guess you will not be here when I get back?" he laughed and walked out. The others did likewise, except for the older man who it seemed did not agree with Ahmed's actions.

"Are you all right now?" he asked tentatively as she still had the knife in her hand.

"Yes thank you, I just need to get dressed. Has this happened before?"

"Yes I am sorry, he thinks it is fun to have sex with a woman when she does not really want it. It is not good, he should not bring women into a house of men, but he does not care; it is his house so we have to as you English say, turn a blind eye."

"Why do these women not report him?"

"They are tourists, too ashamed I suppose, they don't want the hassle, a court case. They would have to stay here, they just want to forget, sometimes they don't even remember what has happened."

Gigliola looked around, the place was a hovel, no furniture just the chair she sat in and the table. No cooker, no fridge, nothing. She asked where the bathroom was, there was no bathroom but a toilet to the right of Ahmed's room. My God, it was disgusting, it looked as if someone had chucked a cow pat down it. The sides were thick with faeces, it was not plumbed in, there was a bucket at the side with water in it. There was no way she was going to sit on that toilet; it was difficult but she used the bucket then tipped it out. When she went back out into the main room her companion said he would go get a coffee for her from Adelina. She thanked him and started to prepare for her escape.

As soon as she knew he had gone, she fastened her blouse, found her shoes and her bag and left, running down the steps so fast she nearly fell to the bottom. She noticed an alley to the left and ran to it, before the man came back out from the cafe. It was like a maze but she eventually found herself on a main road. God she thought she must look a sight. She found a coffee shop and went in, ordered a large Cappuccino and a croissant and then went to the bathroom to straighten herself out. She had a small fold-up brush in her bag so she was able to brush and plait her hair. A little bit of make-up and then she went back to her table. Once her nerves had become less frayed she made a decision, she was afraid to go back to the hotel, Ahmed might show up again, he needed to think she had gone. After her coffee, she rang the hotel and told them she wanted to keep her room, but was going away for a couple of days, if anyone went into the hotel asking for her, they were to say she had gone away and they did not know when or if she would be returning. That sorted, she made her way to the main train station.

She had thought of going to Corleone, but decided she needed somewhere she could relax and get over the ordeal of last night. As she had planned to stay at Cefalu when she first arrived, she decided to take a train there now. She wanted to leave Palermo far behind, she would not get to see Leggio now, would not know the truth, but she had been to Corleone had met her aunt Maria-Antonina even if she had been wary of her. The papers might have covered the story, she no longer really cared, she longed for home, to be safe in the arms of Charlie, to go back to being just Janice Richards, the little known artist. The Mafioso life style was not for her.

The only thing she would thank Leggio for was Yin and Yang who had tried to protect her, but giving them the slip had almost cost her... who knew what? The only regret was that she would never know now just who they really were?

There was an hourly train service to Cefalu, and an intercity train twice a day that went all the way to Milan. That had already left. She decided she just wanted to be on a train, so took the next available one. It was busy, with both local and tourist passengers. She kept herself to herself, managing to get a window seat so she could see the scenery. It was stunning, on her left was the sea, on the right the Sicilian countryside. She already felt more relaxed. It took between 40 to 50 minutes to reach her destination, so it was the middle of the afternoon when she arrived. Not the splendour of Palermo's central station here, more like the local branch lines at home. She could smell the warm sea air as soon as she got off the train. The first thing she needed to do was buy a holdall, but above all else some new clothes.

This town mixed old with new, rather like Palermo. There were brightly coloured buildings like those of Corleone, but then there were modern contemporary ones, Up to date hotels with all the mod cons, swimming pools, saunas and the like. Yes, this was definitely a place to chill out. No Mafia, no Leggio, just Gigliola Richards on holiday. A chance to enjoy Sicily for the beautiful island that it was. She did some shopping then found a trattoria so she could eat. She had decided to look for a small bed and breakfast, something more cosy and personal than a big hotel chain. Once a bed for the night was sorted, she decided to stay in her room, she had bought a bottle of Chardonnay and sat on the balcony of her room looking out at the town, lit up now it was late evening. She had bought herself a swim suit.

Tomorrow she would swim in the sea and wash all the bad memories away.

Fourteen

MORNING CAME AND she dressed and went down for breakfast, there were two other guests, both Germans and both spoke English, so conversation was free flowing. The young man who came to take their orders also spoke good English so it was a win-win situation. Rather than have the usual continental breakfast, she opted for the Sicilian classic Granita, which was a semi-frozen dessert made with ice, sugar and various fruits. She also decided to be not so English by having tea, but instead opted for a 'Granita De Caffe' which was simply coffee with crushed ice. Breakfast over, it was time to hit the beach. She felt as if she had gone back in time to her childhood. When she and Graham were so excited when they went to the seaside, and could run into the sea and splash each other. Here it was stunning, the sea was so blue, the beach a beautiful fawn colour. There were brightly coloured boats pulled away from the water, some upturned The shoreline was like a huge C on its side, at the top of it mountains stood out into the sky from the town in the foreground. Here at the beach's edge, quaint olde worlde houses. It was a good choice to stay in this part of town, away from the modern resort that she assumed was further around the coast. There were few people on the beach so it was tranquil and peaceful, just what she had hoped for. It was good to swim, the waters washing over her, helping to clear her head. After her swim she went and stretched out on the warm sand, and her mind turned to Charlie; she had not rung the house since he had hung up on her; the message on the answerphone made it pretty clear he did not want to speak to her. So she had accepted it, but she did wonder if he regretted that. Was he at home worried sick about her? She spent most of the day at the beach, then decided she should go get changed, find somewhere to eat and maybe explore the night life.

She was a little nervous out at night, especially as she did not have Yin and Yang to watch over her. But she had grown up a hell of a lot since she first arrived on the island. She had also got herself some pepper spray, so if she found herself in a compromising situation she could defend herself. She still cringed when she thought about Ahmed's boss brushing her face with that lecherous look on his. But she had to give other men a chance, they were not all sex mad lunatics, were they? She looked for a wine bar that was fairly quiet. Ordering her usual glass of Chardonnay she found a quiet corner and sat down.

It was not long before she caught someone's eye. A man about her age or just a little older came up and politely asked if he could sit down. At first she was a little apprehensive; he could see this, so went into his jacket pocket and pulled out his wallet. He was an off duty policeman. He almost sensed her relief.

"Please forgive me, I had an unpleasant experience in Palermo."

"Ah the big city, yes I am afraid it is not a safe place for young ladies alone, especially at night."

"It was my own fault really I was too trusting."

"I hope it was not too traumatic?"

"No, it was fine thank you, I am sorry it's Gigliola." She held her hand out, he reciprocated and shook it.

"Antonio." He sat down opposite her.

"You speak very good English, alas I speak lousy Italian." Her attempt at humour.

"It helps, I am ashamed to say I am bilingual, good for the job."

"Do not be ashamed, it's wonderful, I am always envious of people who can speak more than their own language. I always say it is hard for an English person to learn a different language, because we do not learn English we just speak it by copying our parents."

"I had never thought of that before."

"All these verbs and adjectives, I have no idea what they are."

"Maybe I could teach you Italian," he suggested.

She laughed. "I am sorry, is that your chat up line?"

"My colleagues would say that."

"Well it's not so bad, at least we have started a conversation."

"I see you wear a wedding band, is your husband here with you?"

"No, he is at home in England." She fiddled with her ring, would she end up in bed with this man, or would

149

she be faithful to Charlie? With that in mind she only took small sips of her wine, she needed to keep a clear head.

"Don't worry I am not going to jump on you, you're not my type if you get my meaning."

She felt a sense of disappointment, either she got a man who could not wait to abuse her body, or she attracted the attention of a gay man, obviously down on his luck. But it was nice to just have a male friend for once.

That's just what he became. She arranged to meet him for a meal the following day; as she arrived at the wine bar, she saw him sat at a table, he waved to her and upon her arrival got up and politely kissed her on both cheeks, as most Europeans seemed to do.

"Gigliola, please do not be angry with me," Antonio said as she sat down.

"Why would I be angry, are you going to tell me you are not gay after all, and this is a date?"

"No, no I am gay, but there is someone here to see you." He gestured she should look behind her. So she turned around and felt that butterfly sensation. He stood there before her, did not say anything, but took of his shades and put them in his breast pocket.

"I have missed you Gigliola," he said in that sensual voice.

"I think my work here is done. Have a wonderful evening." Antonio got up to excuse himself.

"Thank you Antonio, I am sure we will." Yang tapped Antonio on the back as he turned to leave.

Now there was just the two of them, it was awkward, she had no idea what to say, there was plenty going on in her head. But she could not tell him what she was thinking. Then she found her voice.

"Why are you here, come to tease me again? Get me aroused then slam the door in my face again Mr Mafioso. Just what game are you playing, you think because I almost begged you for sex that now you can have me. When the mood takes you. Just because you know how much I want you."

"No, it's not like that Gigliola. It's not just sex it is something deeper. Hell I don't know. Antonio is a good friend, he said he would help me see you. Away from Palermo, where no one will know where I am. I had to come, ever since I met with you in the hotel. You're in my head, I was so worried when you just disappeared. Let's go for a walk, we can talk then."

"I am not sure I should go anywhere with you."

"I am not going to harm you. I just want to give my body to you. I should not have run away the other night. I was worried I would be missed. When I got home all I could think about was how beautiful your breasts were. How much I wanted to make love to you. You have been in my thoughts ever since. Having to follow you and not being able to hold you, kiss you. It made me very bad tempered. You have had such a profound effect upon me."

Suddenly they both seemed to be more at ease with each other and started a conversation, although she found it hard to concentrate, she just wanted to rip his clothes off. She wanted to feel his lips against hers, to feel his hands caressing her breasts, like he had just before he left, when he so nearly succumbed.

"So do you have a name Mr Mafioso? I nicknamed you 'the undertaker'."

"Ah so you know the Sicilian saying then?"

"I am sorry, what saying?" she asked totally lost.

"Always wear all black, to remind you, not to get on my wrong side, because I am always ready for your funeral."

"Oh that's why certain men in Sicily always dress like you do," she replied.

"As for my name, it is better for us both that you do not know it." He so wished he could tell her, he wanted to hear her whispering it in his ear, he loved her softly spoken English accent. She looked stunning in a light floral dress, it showed her breasts to perfection, he was captivated by them.

"Come let's take a walk on the beach," he gestured she should go first. He did not say very much. She so wanted to ask him if he were a member of the Mafia, but decided against it. Reasoning with herself, as he knew Antonio, he too was probably a policeman. Maybe that was why he could not reveal his name.

When they reached the beach he took off his jacket and laid it on the sand for her to sit on. He told her he knew about her rape. He sounded very angry about it. He sat down next to her, they made eye contact, he leant towards her and kissed her. The flood gates of desire were flung open, and he asked if he could make love to her in the sea. He was so sexy, she did not have a problem with that. She wanted his hands on her body again, to be naked next to him. To look into those beautiful eyes while he took her to his paradise. He took his tie off, removed his shirt and flung it on to the sand. She was spellbound by his firm chest, his skin was so soft, sun tanned and very touchable, as she slid her hands up and down it. She got up, removed her sandals and walked towards the sea. When she reached the shoreline, she stripped naked, and waited, with eager anticipation. He arrived behind her cuddling into her back, his arms around her waist fondling her breasts. She felt his erect penis. He removed his boxer shorts and led her into the warm water of the Mediterranean sea. They kissed and caressed each other's bodies, then he took her to his garden of pleasure. It was so romantic, the gentle rolling of the waves, as they washed over them. Such a magical experience. She could not believe it was really happening.

Antonio had said they could spend the night together at his house, in the guest room. When they arrived, Yang checked with Antonio if it was ok for them to take a shower, because of the sand. They showered together and continued on from where they had left off when leaving the sea. It was like falling off a cloud into a lake of passion. He knew just what to do to make her whole body tingle. They went from the shower to the bedroom. They made love.

"God you're one hell of a lover; then I knew you would be. My whole body feels so alive. Thank you Yang for giving in, for letting the passion consume you."

"Why do you call me Yang?"

"I call you and your friend Yin and Yang. You're the sexy masculine man, so you had to be Yang."

"I wish I could be honest with you, and tell you who I am, put I can't. If this gets out that I have slept with you, I will be in big trouble but I don't care." He kissed her again and caressed her breasts. She sat on top of him and gyrated her hips on his genitals, to try to instigate a response.

"Oh Gigliola I so want to have you again, but at the

moment the body will not allow it."

"I will bring the big man out of his slumber, so we can go to paradise yet again."

"God I wish it was that easy, but I have performed more than once tonight, we should sleep."

"Sleep? I want you inside of me again, thrusting into me, making my whole body tingle with passion and desire." She continued to gyrate her hips. It eventually had the desired effect and they made love again. His hands sliding up and down her body, caressing her breasts. His tongue licking her skin sending her into sexual orbit. God it had been worth the wait. She had cried when he left her hotel room, sure he would not give in to his desire for her. But he had.

"I am possessive, I will not want you to fuck anyone else. Your body is mine now, mine to worship, mine to take you to paradise, so you will never want to leave. Will you go home and make love to your wife?"

"Gigliola, I am not married, nor do I have a girlfriend. I am your's for as long as you desire me. But my beautiful sexy mistress, I must get some sleep. You are insatiable but after some rest, I shall do all I can to change that." He kissed her, and closed his eyes. They must have fallen asleep. It was light, she opened her eyes turned over to touch him, but he was not there. On his pillow was a note.

He shattered her romantic vision by saying it should not have happened. But he was glad it had. It had been wonderful. Saying he was sure that what had taken place between them would remain firmly to the front of his mind for days. That she had made him feel so alive with passion and sexual desire. Then he turned the screw, when he told her she must not try to speak to, or approach him. To do so could put them both in danger. She got dressed and went out into the lounge. Antonio was watching the news.

"Are you OK?" He could tell she wasn't.

"He just sneaked out, it was beautiful at the beach. Such a magical night. But he had what he wanted. He is no different from the rest. Just wanted to boost his ego, by having Leggio's alleged daughter." She began to cry. This was new territory for Antonio, he got flustered, then thought damn it, she needed a hug.

"My sweet lady, believe me he is not like that; He could not say anything to anyone else. But he has thought of nothing else but you since you went to Ansa. He trusts me, he knows I will not go shooting my mouth off. He said you had awakened feelings within him that no other woman has done before. He would be so upset to see you like this, he really is a gentle soul."

"No, he just wanted an ego trip, did it excite him I wonder, going with an English woman? Then he knows I am Sicilian. All this crap about not being able to talk to him, because it will put me in danger. My God I fell for it. I should have known a good looking guy like that would not really want to screw me. It was just a game for him. Did they have a bet who would get their hands down my pants first? I am sorry Antonio that he used you like this, the bastard." She found her bag, put her sandals on, and left.

Antonio went to the phone.

"Hey it's me. She was very upset, even crying, I had to comfort her. Yeh, I think the only woman I have ever hugged is my mother. Why did you just leave like that?

Did you not think how it would look? She thinks you were just on an ego trip, bad news for you mate. Better hope she does not create a scene, if this gets back to the boss, I would be on the next train to Milan if I were you. I will try and calm her down, explain to her. I would suggest you send her some flowers, but the mood she is in at the moment, she would want to hit you with them! I must go, I will let you know how it pans out. She is going back to Palermo on Sunday, I know where she is staying, I will have a word with her. You owe me big time. Ciao."

After work he stopped off at the bed and breakfast Gigliola was staying at, but she was not there. He drove home, and decided to try the beach. He was in luck, she was sitting on the sand just staring out to sea.

"Gigliola, I hoped I would find you."

She turned and looked at him. Her eyes were red, she had been crying again.

"I hate him, why did he do this to me? I have been married four years, never once have I looked at another man. Then he waltzed in with his beautiful brown eyes, and I broke my marriage vows. Do you know what's so bloody sad, my own husband has brown eyes, but they are nothing like his. I cannot get him out of my head. Then I guess that's what he wanted. How many women in Palermo wish they could get back into his bed. I was just another notch on the bedpost as we say in England."

"He asked me to give you this, he is desperate to explain why he left like he did. It is not what you think, he has true feelings for you. He so wants to see you again but it would have to be in secret." He held a small note out to her. She snatched it from his hand and ripped it up.

"Take it back to him, I don't want his pathetic excuses. Now leave me alone." She started to cry again, this man had such a profound effect on her. She knew deep down they had shared something really special, but his underhanded departure had tarnished it.

"Hey come on, just because he is a prat. Don't let him spoil our friendship, there was so much we were going to do. Places I said I would show you. Forget him, let's sweep it under the carpet, and enjoy your last day or so having fun. What do you say?"

"I say you are a wonderful man, kind and considerate, and yes you are right. It is not the first bad experience I have had while I have been here." She wiped her face and gave one of her deep sighs.

He smiled and laughed. "From what I heard, it did not sound like a bad experience."

"Oh my God, were we noisy?" She started to blush.

"I could not possibly comment. That's better, you have a lovely smile. Come I will do you a feast, seafood, with some salad, and a nice cold white wine." He held out his hand and helped her to get up. They had a great evening, it was as if nothing had taken place with the 'Mystery Man'.

When it was time to leave he kissed her two cheeks, hugged her and went on to say she must ring to let him know she had arrived home safely. He also said she must return for a holiday with Charlie, they would both be most welcome. He saw her onto the train back to Palermo, and stayed to wave her off.

Her flight from Punta Raisa was not until the morning so, as she was still booked in at the President, she took a taxi to the hotel.

"Miss Richards, so glad you are back to stay with us. Did you find Cefalu pleasing?" The duty manager welcomed her from the reception desk.

"Oh yes such a beautiful place, is there nowhere in Sicily that is not so beautiful?"

"I am sad to say that yes, as you have seen here in Palermo there are places where poverty and despair... Oh forgive me, I do not want to spoil your image of our beautiful island." He handed the key to her and she went up to her room. She made some tea, and had another cry.

After her tea, she decided to have a walk up to the prison; she wondered if she had not disappeared to Cefalu would she have got in to see Leggio? Now she would never know. She didn't go too near the main gates, not wanting another round with a heavily armed policeman. She had seen Leggio on the TV, she had pictures from the papers, she had at least met Maria-Antonina, so it had not all been bad. Now it was time to leave Leggio and the Mafia here on this island. As the saying went 'what you have never had, you never miss'. She had never known Leggio as her father, never heard of him until her mother's death, so she would not miss him now. When she got home she would burn everything, the name Gigliola would be confined to a trash bin, she was Janice Richards, once Walters; Archie had adopted her, given her his name, and she was damn well going to be proud of it. As she walked back to the hotel she was sure she saw Yin and Yang, but when she looked again she saw no one. Maybe she had just wanted to see them one last time. She went in, had a bath, then slipped between the cool cotton sheets. Tomorrow she was flying home, just before she closed her eyes, she whispered 'Goodnight

Luciano' and wondered would she ever return to Sicily?

Morning came all too soon, and it was time to go back home, back to reality. She had got a small gift for Maria, who had been more than just a maid to her. Having found her hard at work as always, she gave her the ornately wrapped gift. Maria was thrilled, and got emotional; that set Gigliola off and they hugged and cried at the same time.

"I will miss you Maria, thank you, thank you for being a friend, I hope it was not because you were fearful of my father." She thought if Charlie had been there he would have chastised her, and said 'You had to mention him didn't you? You couldn't help yourself'.

Maria assured her it had nothing to do with who her father might be.

That stung her a little bit, and she realised she was not going to forget Leggio that easily.

Time was marching on and she needed to leave for the airport, she double checked her room once more then went down to settle her bill.

"So Miss Richards, the time has come for you to leave. I am sorry you could not get in to see your father, maybe you can come again before he returns to Sardinia."

"You never know. It has been quite an experience, my first time abroad, maybe I might just stay at home."

She smiled at the manager who had come to see her off, maybe he wanted to make sure she was really going this time. He smiled back and walked her out to the taxi. She glanced across the road, there they were, in their immaculate suits, with their fancy mirrored shades. She waved at them, but there was no response. So she got in the taxi and headed for the airport.

This was the bit she hated, the waiting around, she knew what she would do. Taking out a small sketch pad from her large shoulder bag, she decided to draw. To put down on paper the images of Sicily she had in her head, before they faded too much. She found herself drawing Ahmed, but in a macabre way. She shuddered when she relived what he had done to her, would have done to her, had she not come round and realised what was about to happen. She seemed to be channelling her emotions into the drawing. She could not bare to continue with it and decided instead to do her interpretation of Corleone. Maybe when she got home she would paint it properly and send it to Luciano? She smiled, had she not told herself that when she got home this would all be dead and buried, yet here she was making plans to send him one of her paintings. Time had marched on with her being so preoccupied and it was time to go through customs. She put her pad and pencil back in her bag and got up to go towards the gates that took passengers into the security area.

It was then she noticed him. There was no mistake, she knew it was Yang. She wondered why they were both not there, then in the confines of the airport, there was more than an adequate amount of security, so maybe they did not both need to be there, to see she actually got on the plane. There seemed to be a lot of people who were eager to see her leave.

As she made her way across the concourse he walked towards her. She suddenly felt afraid; what was going to happen? So she stopped and waited to see what would transpire. He stood in front of her, lifted his shades and once again she saw his deep brown eyes. She felt that sensation in her stomach. What did she do?

"So you came to make sure I got on the plane?" She tried to sound angry but it was futile.

"You would not answer my notes, did not ring me. I had to see you before you left. Please let me feel those lips against mine just once more. So I relive that beautiful moment when we shared love in the sea." He walked up to her, took her case from her hand, placed it on the floor, then he flung his arms around her and kissed her, it was long and lingering. They shared a last moment of passion.

"Arrivederci Gigliola." With that he turned around and walked away.

She stood there transfixed on him as she watched him disappear into the crowds of other passengers. Then she jolted back to reality when she was nearly knocked over by a luggage trolley.

"Scusi" the offending passenger said.

She smiled and nodded her head, then realised she needed to go get her bags checked. It was when she got her passport out that the small piece of paper fell on to the desk. She picked it up and looked at it. It read 'I have fallen in love with you. Ring me'. Why had she not seen this before, how did it get into her bag? Antonio, the Sicilian matchmaker.

She wanted to turn around, go back, go back and tell him she had not seen it. He had wanted to communicate with her. That was why he came alone. He must have felt she had shunned him. Her eyes were darting around for a telephone kiosk. But it was pointless trying to ring him, he would be on his way back into the city. Once she had looked into those eyes, he had caught her in his aura yet again. At this very moment in time, she yearned for him, she wanted him, wanted them to both be back in the sea, that had been so magical. She knew he had got inside her head and she was sure he would be for a long while yet. It seemed she had totally misjudged him, now it was too late. She wanted to cry, God, that damned man, all he did to her at present was make her cry. Should she turn round and go back? He was friends with Fabio; he could tell him she had not gone home after all. But they would have to sneak around, no she did not want any harm to come to him. She would always have that wonderful memory. The knowledge that a man so handsome, so bloody sexy, had wanted to make love to her, had fallen for her.

It was soon time to get on the plane; as she walked up to the aircraft's door, she had one last look around at Sicily. Would she ever come here again? She did not know, if she did would she be alone to contact him, or would Charlie be with her? If alone, would her arrival mean Yin and Yang would once again follow her every move?

It would not take long to get back to London; once settled in her seat, she took a long drink of water then closed her eyes.

She was back in the bedroom at Antonio's house, they stood facing each other, she took his shades off, and folding them put them into the pocket of his jacket, she then slowly slid that from his shoulders and threw it to the floor. She put her finger to his mouth to tell him not to speak. Then after removing his tie, she unbuttoned his silk shirt, but did not take it off. Instead she took her dress off, removed her bra, then pushed her breasts into his chest, kissing his neck, she could almost smell his sensuality. He took his shirt off, she again caressed his beautiful honed chest. Then standing there in her briefs, she undid his thick leather belt, unzipped his trousers and allowed them to slip to the floor; he pushed his shoes off and stepped out of his trousers. She momentarily stepped back so she could see his boxers, the big bulge told her he was aroused, he was ready to take her to his sexual paradise, she ripped her briefs off and stood before him naked,

He removed his own underwear, and that was it, they laid on the bed and made passionate love, she orgasmed, something she had never done with Charlie. It was beautiful, his soft Sicilian voice calling her Gigliola over and over. She never wanted it to end, but it did, thanks to the air stewardess who had nudged her to say she needed to put her seat belt on, they would be landing shortly. She opened her eyes, rubbed her face and gave a deep sigh. It had been so beautiful, and now she had found out he was in love with her.

All the way back into London that's all she could think about, making love to this Mafioso, but was he? She still did not know just who he was. Did it matter, did it really matter, those eyes, the way he had looked at her, yes for the briefest of moments. But they had said more than words could ever say. She thought about Charlie, how could she have sex with him now; he could not compete with this policeman/Mafioso she had in her head. What if she started to shout Yang, Charlie would know then that something had happened in the warm Sicilian sun. She shook her head, that blasted note, why had Antonio not put it somewhere else, so she would have seen it before she left. What if she rang him now? But he had kissed her at the airport, he knew by her response the passion was still there, that they could have made it work. But what of Charlie? She was a married woman, maybe it was fate that meant she did not see the note until it was too late. Now she would never know what might have been.

Fifteen

SHE HAD TO put all the whats and ifs to one side and concentrate on reaching Kings Cross without getting herself run over. The good thing about being back in Blighty meant she could get a decent cup of tea. She was feeling hungry so went into the station cafe for tea and a good old English sausage roll. Then as she had got the coach to the airport, she went to the ticket office so she could get the next train back to York. She had about 30 minutes, so decided she would ring Charlie at the office. Let him know she was on her way home.

"Good afternoon, Architects by Design, how can I help you? Hello Mrs Richards."

"Is Charlie in the office or on site?"

"No Mrs Richards, he is here, one moment please."

Those few seconds seemed like an eternity, but she was relieved when she heard Charlie's voice.

"Janice, thank God you're ok."

"Yes I am fine, I never rang again, after the terse

message."

"Oh honey, I am so sorry about that, I said it in haste, I was drunk, angry, lonely, but that's no excuse, I am just so happy to hear your voice."

"I am at Kings Cross, train is about to leave in 20 minutes, I should arrive in York just after five."

"You want me to come and pick you up?" He was eager to see her.

"No, no, I have got a ticket straight through to Harrogate. I will see you when I get home." She put the telephone down, she couldn't talk anymore, he had just popped back into her head. She again threw her hands up to her face, she seemed to be doing a lot of that, and the deep sighs. Once on the train, she tried to carry on with the drawing she had started at Punta Raisa, but it was no use, she kept seeing those eyes, that look, 'oh my God' she said under her breath, what was she going to do? Then what could she do?

Once back in Harrogate she got a taxi from the train station. Charlie was at the door to greet her.

"Wow, look at you, a sun tan suits you." He rushed to kiss her, but she turned away. So he just took her bags and didn't make anything of it.

"Tea, nothing like a cup of tea in your own cup. Yes?"

"Yes please, the tea on the train and the price they charge, it wouldn't be so bad if they made sure the water was hot." She went and sat in the lounge, Charlie had obviously run the Hoover around, everywhere looked pristine.

He came in with a tray and the teapot. "Thought you might want more than just one cup"

"Thank you."

"So what was it like?" He slid over the couch arm to sit down.

"Hot, it was so hot, I thought I would spend the week sat in the bath, but Fabio was right, you soon get used to it." She waited for Charlie to ask, and he did.

"Fabio?"

"Yes, he worked at the hotel, I was going to stay at Cefalu, I thought it was just down the road, turned out it was a good few miles away. So I ended up at a hotel opposite the entrance to the port." She sipped her tea.

"You don't seem all that keen to talk about it?"

"It's been a long day, all the travelling, I just want a nice bath with some Radox and an early night."

"Ok, if you're sure you don't want anything to eat. I could do you something, how about some scrambled eggs and bacon? I bet you have lost weight. What did you eat?"

"Breakfast was not so bad, cereal and fruit, and they have this beautiful dish like a pudding called Granita, like ice cream with bits of fruit in it, very sugary, they like sugary things. I even became quite accustomed to coffee, especially Cappuccino. Would you believe?" She replenished her cup with some more tea; she tried to be attentive, but Yang was there flashing in front of her eyes, standing with his partner watching her from behind his shades.

"Janice, are you all right, you seem miles away?"

"Yes, sorry, just thinking how lucky I am."

"In what respect?"

"Well I am here. I heard and read about some terrible things Luciano did, when he was younger. I find it hard to comprehend just what I thought I was doing. Like you said I could have been coming home on that plane in a body bag." She suddenly felt a chill and decided she needed her bath to warm her up, the climate change had been more of a shock then she had thought it would be.

So she left Charlie and went upstairs. She managed to hold it together until she got in the bath. Then she just started to cry, no idea why, was it relief, or was she crying for her 'mysterious man'? But she had not really known him, she was fixated she was sure with who he was, she wanted him to be a Mafioso, but like Luciano they were faceless killers, look how baby-faced Luciano had been, photos of him as a young man, shirt and tie, he looked ok. Besides not all of them would go around blowing people's brains out. He might be a great guy, just a driver, then again he could be a policeman. Would she fantasise about him any less if he were? She started to relax, the warm water soothing her soul as she washed her hair. She checked her skin, it still showed the bite marks from that flea ridden mattress at the hovel Ahmed called home. She had cream to help treat it, at least now it did not itch so much. The bruises were slowly fading on her breasts. What would Charlie say when he saw them, would he believe her explanation. Then how she felt at the moment, would she want him close enough to see?

She awoke to Charlie opening the curtains and pulling across the bedside table, he had made her breakfast in bed.

"I thought I would spoil you; you didn't have a very good night, it was almost as if you were having a night-mare, you seemed to be running away from someone."

"That's very odd, did I bother you?"

"No, I just woke you up and then you seemed fine."

Janice had worried about this happening, ever since that fateful night at Ahmed's house she had suffered with night terrors. She had no idea how or if she wanted to talk to Charlie about it. How might he react if he found out she had almost been raped? Hell she had only been home a few hours, most of that asleep, things like that could wait. She had hoped to dream about her Sicilian lover, she so wished she knew his name.

"Tuck in, I have to say this last week I have become quite handy in the kitchen, I think you will find your scrambled eggs are done to your liking madam."

"Oh Charlie it is good to be home. You would have loved Cefalu, it was beautiful, swimming in the sea."

"I hope you took photographs?"

"Um just a few." She laughed and had a bite of her toast.

"I am sorry but I have to go into work for a bit, but then I will be home and we can spend the day together. Is that ok?"

It was more than ok with her, it meant she could ring Sicily, she had decided last night while she was in the bath that she needed to explain why she had not rung him, that she was not still mad at him. It was mid morning which meant it would be nearly lunch time in Palermo, would he be there? Wherever the telephone was.

"Is that Antonio's friend?" she asked.

"Yes"

"It's Gigliola." She waited for his response.

"Gigliola you have called me," he said surprised.

"I never saw the telephone number until I was going through customs, it fell out of my bag when I got my passport out."

"That's a shame Gigliola."

"I love the way you say my name."

"So are you missing me?" he asked in a seductive tone, that gave her goose bumps.

"Can you tell me your name now I am no longer in Palermo?"

"It is Salvatore. Gigliola, you can call me whatever you want, but I would like to think I would still be called your lover. I do believe we are going to flirt down the line," he said in that soft Sicilian tone he had.

"Salvatore is a beautiful name, you are a very handsome man, with your come to bed eyes. I can't stop thinking about you, I keep seeing us in the sea."

"Do we make love again?" he said wistfully.

"Yes, it's the most wonderful sex I have ever had."

"Ah but it is just a dream Gigliola, a dream now, a memory, but you can always come back, I meant what I said in my note, I have fallen in love with you, I wish you would come home, come back to me," he said almost pleading.

"I very nearly did that, then I thought it might not be a good idea."

"Why was that?" he sounded intrigued.

"With you being a Mafioso. Maybe one of my father's men?" She waited for his response, what would he say?

"Oh you think I am a Mafioso and work for Leggio?" He gave a seductive laugh.

"You dress like one, I must say I loved the silk shirt, but I adored what was inside. Then you know that. I so wanted to ask you if you were in the Mafia, but thought you could be a policeman Like Antonio."

"If you want me to be a Mafioso, I will be."

"Does that mean you're not?"

"Would it matter?"

"No I just want to undress you and make love to you, I wanted that night to never end... Oh I am sorry, Salvatore I am..."

She suddenly looked round and saw Charlie standing in the doorway.

"Gigliola?"

"I am sorry I have to go."

"Can I ring you?"

"No, no Antonio ciao." She hoped the fact she had used that name would signal to him that she had company. So he hung up.

"Charlie, I thought you were at the office."

"So who is bloody Antonio, had a holiday romance after all did we, sea sun and sex."

"Please Charlie it's not like that at all." She was mortified; how much of the conversation had he heard?

"Seemed pretty steamy from what I heard. Silk shirt and the like."

"It's not what you think. The first time I spoke to Antonio was as I was going into security, at the airport. He took his shades off and just said 'Goodbye Gigliola'; end of story."

"No no, there is more to it than that. You really should remember his name, is it Antonio or Salvatore?"

"Look I got off the ferry, booked in the hotel, had breakfast, went to the prison, then I saw them, two men following me, dark suits, ties fancy shades. Wherever I went they were there. I told the journalists about them, they said they could be police, just keeping an eye on me. Personally I thought they were Mafioso, Leggio's men.

171

I felt safe knowing they were there. I can prove this is true, when I have my photos developed, I can show you them. After I had seen the journalists I sat in a garden, they naturally followed me there, I ate some seafood, it was so hot they got themselves an ice cream. I thought it was funny so against the stereotype of a Mafioso, an ice cream and not a gun in their hand, I took a photo of them both, they turned away from the camera but they are there."

"You have been so distant since you came back, what am I to think?"

"I haven't been back 24 hours yet, give me a break. I just wanted Antonio to know I got home all right, so whoever had employed him and the other one to follow me would know I was fine."

"Guess it does make sense. But you sounded as if you were flirting with him."

"It's just the way they talk, just a bit of banter, I mean come on he is over 1,000 miles away, it's not as if I can pop in the car and go to meet him, is it?"

"Fair point. Sorry, just jealous I guess."

She started to laugh.

"What's so funny?"

"I never thought I would hear you say you were jealous of a Mafioso. You can always start dressing like him, a silk shirt might suit you." She regretted saying that. It would be just like Charlie to go buy one. But that was what Salvatore wore, no it would sully her memory of him, it would tarnish her memory. She had told Salvatore not to call her, she realised she had to be strong. She must do like wise and not call him. She should view it as a holiday romance, although it never had been. Her time in Sicily was finished now, time to let go, get back to normal. Tomorrow she would return to her studio, she had so many ideas whirling around in her head, she would not have time to think about him. But she could not guarantee he would not be in her dreams!

Charlie seemed more content now she had explained more. He had not done much shopping so they had a light lunch and then went to the supermarket to stock up. He said he wanted to show Janice what a good cook he was now, by doing Beef Wellington for their evening meal. He offered to buy a bottle of Sicilian wine as a peace offering, but Janice said she had drunk enough of that and a nice South African red would be just the job.

They ate at seven, then retired to the lounge. Charlie said he would like to hear about her trip. He had thought long and hard all week about the way he had been, and he was sorry he had not supported her as well as he could have.

She decided to condense her stay in Sicily to the good parts, she did not really want to remember the bad, the 'greasy Itis' as Charlie referred to them. Most of the men she had encountered were friendly, polite and respectful. There had just been four bad eggs in the basket, the one with the greatest stench like his toilet had been Ahmed. She should have reported him, but she had no proof, and in the end Salvatore and his companion had dealt with him with their own brand of justice.

She told Charlie about the irate soldier with the massive machine gun, whatever it was. How he only looked about 12 but was still scary. How she had been taken to Corleone, how the people had treated her as if she was

English Royalty or some American celebrity. She felt quite emotional when she told him about Maria-Antonina, Luciano's sister. How she had acknowledged her in her own way. Then she told him about Antonio, who turned out to be a policeman and had been assigned to watch over her when she stayed in Cefalu, on who's orders he did not say. The wonderful time she had swimming in the sea, the beautiful buildings, statues everywhere. Then she told him about the dark side of Palermo, the slums, the derelict buildings, those that had, and those that had not. Highlighted by the expensive yachts moored in the Marina. How many of them belonged to Mafioso bought on the back of the misery they inflicted on the honest working people of Palermo, and elsewhere on the Island.

"I have noticed bite marks, your skin looks red and irritated." Charlie lifted her sleeve to look.

"Yes, mosquitoes but I have cream to cope with it. The hotel they spray the rooms, but outside you're at their mercy." She had tried to sound casual about it, it must have been convincing as Charlie changed the subject. He asked her what Italian TV was like. She said she never really bothered with it, sometimes she would catch a bit of the news; she had seen Leggio in the court room housed in a big metal cage, which she said was the best way to describe it.

Charlie was not worried but he was shocked that she did not talk so much about her trip. He still had it in the back of his mind that there was something she was hiding from him. He kept going back to the telephone call, that bugged him, he was sure she had not been totally honest about this Mafioso guy. Before she left she had been obsessive, maybe she had wanted to sleep with such a man, for the thrill of it all. The adrenaline rush, like those idiots that liked jumping into the sea off cliff tops for that intense thrill. He would keep his cool, then after he had seen her so called photographic evidence, make up his mind whether or not to ask her straight out, had she slept with him?

They had gone to bed, and Janice seemed to be sleeping. Charlie had caught his wife's problem, he could not get this bloody Antonio guy out of his head, he saw them making love, it was passionate, all he could see in his mind's eye was this guy mauling his wife, screaming her name Gigliola while he thrust almost violently within her. He was jolted from this vision by Janice, who had started to talk in her sleep. He watched as she got out of bed, went to the dressing table took her hairbrush and then sat on the dressing table chair. Waving the brush from side to side.

"Come near me and I will kill you, I mean it, I will stab you to death you bastard."

Charlie knew he had not to try and wake her, it could be more dangerous, so he just sat at the end of the bed and watched her.

"You drugged me didn't you? I will tell Yin and Yang, they will sort you out."

Why was she waving the hair brush? Then he realised whenever this incident had occurred she must have had a knife in her hand. But where was she and why if she had been truthful about the mysterious men, were they not there? So where were they? Her two knights in shining armour. Had she trusted them, not knowing the reason they were following her was not because they were looking out for her, but wanted to harm her? Was this why she would not talk about her trip, was it too traumatic for her to relive? Then he realised that wasn't right; she had said their names, used them to scare her attacker. He so wanted to help her get out of the nightmare she was having, but could only sit and wait until she woke up herself.

It was light when she did and saw Charlie on the bed looking at her. She looked down at her hands, saw the brush and dropped it onto the floor.

"Will you tell me about it now?" Charlie pleaded with her. "Oh honey, you're shaking, can I come and hold you, I promise I won't hurt you?"

She nodded her head, as soon as they made contact she started to cry, she sobbed uncontrollably, at last allowing herself to deal with the horror of that night.

"Shall I make you some tea first?"

"No, don't leave me."

"Ok, come and sit down next to me on the bed"

She went on to tell Charlie how Ahmed had gained her confidence, never once tried to make a pass at her, knowing all the time how he was going to sleep with her. His companion had told her he was not a fisherman but a drug dealer, for Toto Riini. Of course she knew only too well who he was, once her father's loyal foot soldier, but then there was no loyalty in the Mafia and everyone eventually wanted to be the boss. Ahmed had used some of his drugs to spike her drink. She started to come round when...

"It's ok, I don't need to hear any more." He could see the fear for himself, and he knew anyway what she was going to say, but she said it anyway. Maybe just glad to be able to tell someone.

"Charlie, he was going to rape me. He was like an animal. I thought he was going to bite my nipples off!"

"Sweetheart, come on you're safe now, but what the hell happened to 'Yin and bloody Yang', where the hell were they?"

"Ahmed was clever, he knew he had to shake them off somehow. I think that's why he chose the cafe. The back door went into a big square, it had buildings all around with a few alleyways, a bit like York. They will have waited outside the cafe."

"Expecting you to leave the way you went in," Charlie said finishing her sentence.

"I am sure by the time they realised, it was too late. I eventually got the chance to run away. This is what he did to me." She pulled her slip up and showed him the bruises on her breasts.

"The bastard."

She managed a brief smile.

"Yes, they must have sent word out that I was floating around somewhere. Luckily for me I ended up in Cefalu and met Antonio. Oh my God, Antonio, I promised to ring him when I got home." Janice jumped up, Charlie stopped her.

"Hey it's only 6am, the poor guy is probably not at work yet. You need some sleep, I will go make you a cup of camomile tea, it will help calm your stress levels and help you relax."

"Yes, that sounds like a good idea."

"I want you in the bed dreaming, dreaming of when you were swimming in the sea, OK?"

"Yes, it was so beautiful at Cefalu. I am so glad I went there and not to Corleone." He had no idea it would not be swimming she would be dreaming about, it would be her Mafioso making love to her in that warm sea water, with the gentle waves splashing them, how sexy he looked when his hair was wet!

Charlie watched her sleeping for a while, then decided he would ring Antonio for her, he felt guilty because he was starting to wonder, if Antonio was the one she might have slept with. Of course he was not to know, there was more chance of him getting between the sheets with him, than her. Why did he not just trust her? She had never strayed, never looked as if she wanted too. He decided, no he did trust her, she could ring herself when she got up to have something to eat.

When she did get up Charlie asked her if she wanted to see the doctor, maybe some sleeping pills might be a good idea. Janice said that now she had talked about what had happened, she would probably not have any more problems sleeping. He agreed if she was sure. Looking in her bag she took out her address book, Charlie watched this, he said he was going to trust his wife, but that little voice in his head still bothered him. Would Salvatore or whatever his bloody name was, would his number be in there? Janice went to the phone, she was not gone long, and suddenly became quite hysterical as she came running into the lounge.

"They killed him, they killed him, the bastards killed him."

She was in such a state, Charlie had no option but to slap her hard across the face. That did the trick.

"So who is dead?"

She glared at Charlie.

"You won't care, I bet you have been thinking I slept

178

with him."

His look said it all.

"My God you did."

"Well if it was not that Salvatore guy."

"I went to Sicily to find out about my father, not to get laid."

"What, you would have turned it down, if it had been one of your precious Mafioso?"

"Don't be clever Charlie, it does not suit you."

"So are you going to tell me, or do I have to guess. Oh no not your Mafioso." Charlie was being flippant. He could not help it, he was so bloody jealous of this blasted Sicilian goon.

"He was such a lovely man, they couldn't get to Leggio, so they got to me, through him"

"Who for fuck's sake Janice? Cut the bloody drama, who the hell is dead?"

"Antonio, Antonio, they killed him, the police station said he was dead."

"Huh, did they actually come out and say the Mafia had killed him? Or is it possible, this is only an idea, that as a policeman, he could have died in some other way, or that he might have been in a car crash, an accident that resulted in him dying?"

"Oh go to hell." She got up from the floor, grabbed her bag and left the house, slamming the front door so hard the glass cracked.

"Oh nice one Janice." Charlie shouted after her as she opened her car door.

She drove to her studio and went straight to the phone, started to dial but then put the receiver down, before she changed her mind again and this time dialled the whole number.

"Salvatore?"

"What would you say if it wasn't?" he replied.

"Check I had dialled the right number."

"Gigliola, I wondered if you would ring again."

"How could I not, I tried not to."

"Erm, so you don't have much willpower then?"

"Not when it comes to you."

"Oh so are we going to have another steamy phone call?"

"Would you like that?"

"What I would really like is for you to jump on a plane and come back to Sicily. Would you do that for me?"

"Oh, I have only just come home."

"Yes but I am missing you."

"How can you be? You don't know me, like I do not know you. We are both just trapped in a few hours when we shared our bodies, became as one."

"Ouch Gigliola, you wound me, I know far more about you than you think. Oh and don't you dare say it."

"Say what?"

"No you are not going to get me to say it either, you must believe what you want."

"I know, you're a spy really. That's all subterfuge pretending to be something you're not."

"You have an over-active imagination Gigliola. So what does your imagination conjure up about me now?"

"All right, I can see your face now, you're not just the guy with the fancy shades, beautiful as they are. I remember now that really hot day, after I had been to Ansa. You and Yin followed me into that little garden, because it was so hot, you didn't have your jackets or your ties on, looking very casual. You had that silk shirt on, two of your buttons unfastened so I could see some of your neck."

"It aroused you sexually?"

"Yes, I sat there and imagined your shirt was opened to the waist, I could see your chest, you obviously worked out, or went to the gym."

"Maybe it's all those dead bodies I move?"

"Wow you cracked a joke."

"I can be funny, as well as sexy."

"Vain as well."

"Oh no no no Gigliola, you were the one that said I was sexy."

"Point taken. Anyway getting back to my fantasy, we were no longer in the garden, there was just you and I. I undressed you, my eyes were captivated by your bum."

"My bottom."

"Yes well rounded and firm, I could feel my hands squeezing it gently, then I pulled your boxers down, and saw...

He interrupted her, "Did you like what you saw?"

"No, I thought my God is that it?" She started to laugh.

"Well, that's that then."

"I'm sorry, of course I liked what I saw."

"Look Gigliola I have had an idea, if you won't come back to Sicily, I will come across to the UK and bring you back home."

"You would do that, just to have sex with me?"

"Gigliola, is that how you see me? When I looked at you with my eyes, not through my shades, I knew you were the woman I wanted to be with. That first time I

181

was close to you when I opened the door at the wine bar, I knew. But I could not say anything. I had a job to do."

"So you are a Mafioso."

"Mafia Mafia Mafia, that's all you go on about, what about me as a person, forget the Mafia, it's me and you Gigliola, not Leggio, not the sodding 'Godfather'. I am in love with you, God knows why, because the only thing you love is the bloody Mafia. Look, when you have decided what you really want, ring me." He rang off.

She put the phone down, she was stunned, where had all that come from? She had seen a side of him she did not like, he was just like her father, a hot head. God she almost felt sorry for Ahmed, if he could lose it like that, he must have really given that poor sod a right beating. Suddenly she did not see the sensual-talking Sicilian anymore. He had blown that wonderful image of himself out of the water. This was karma's way of telling her, she was well rid of him; she had Charlie, she didn't need Salvatore, he could go to hell for all she cared. But she couldn't help wondering why he sounded off like he did. Was he disillusioned with the Mafia, did he see her as a way to leave it, but could you ever leave the Mafia? Had he wanted to use her to escape the horrors he might have seen? Now he would never get that chance. He had blown it, she felt a little tear fall down her cheek. She had not wanted it to end like this.

Sixteen

IT TOOK HER along time, but she finally put Salvatore into the vault of her mind. To make sure he could not reappear, she destroyed all photographs she had of him, so the temptation to take a sly peek did not present itself. She and Charlie muddled along, they were more like house mates, than man and wife. Something that frustrated her, she wanted to be as he had once said, 'the dutiful wife', but she also wanted to be the one that fulfilled his sexual desires. After all this time she still did not know if he had a mistress, once upon a time she would not have cared, but now she did. She had turned the love she thought she had for the other man into a deep love for Charlie. But all he seemed to do was slam the door in her face. She couldn't recall what prompted it, but he suddenly started talking about Liggio again.

"Don't you ever wonder how your father is doing, I heard he is not so well" he slipped it into conversation while they ate.

"I'm sorry, did you just say Liggio?"

"Well, that is the name of your father, and I wondered would it not be prudent to change your name back to what it should be."

"You're not serious?" she couldn't believe what she had just heard.

"Of course I am serious, it might help you get to see him."

"Why the hell would I want to do that."

"Because."

"Because, because what, Archie was my father, he gave me his name, I am proud of who I am, I do not need to be Gigliola Bloody Liggio." there was suddenly silence. It had been when she said her Italian name, her mind had computed the files and brought out Salvatore.

"Are you alright?" for once he seemed genuinely concerned. "I'll get you some water"

"No, I am fine, just go away leave me alone. Four years it has taken me to put all that behind me. I wanted to forget, for us to get on with our lives, to love each other again, as we once did before the whole nightmare started. She just looked at him and shook her head.

She just sat there staring at her plate. She so wanted to scream Salvatore's name so bloody loud, that the whole street would hear her. She had got over him by convincing herself he was dead, that he deserved that because he was not really a nice man, he was a member of the Mafia, he probably worked for her alleged father, she didn't care. Oh, but she did, she had shut him away, thought the key was lost. Then that bloody idiot of a husband, not only finds the key but gives it to her. So here she was going back into the loop again. Still there was a good side, she had nothing to remind her of his physical appearance, she had destroyed all trace of him. She recalled how she slowly forgot his name, wanting to call him Flavio, . There had been times when she felt as if the whole thing had been a dream, that she had not been to Palermo, because it all seemed so bizarre. Now thanks to Charlie she had to accept it was all real, and she was still no nearer the truth. She had been under so much pressure. She finished her wine and cleared the table. When she went into the lounge Charlie was sprawled on the couch watching nothing really, he had the television on, but did not seem all that interested.

"Look Janice, how can we move on with this hanging over our heads, I am sorry I could have broached it differently."

"Why, bring it up at all."

"Look at us, look at our marriage, it's a farce, its painful to be in."

"Well, we know the answer then don't we, we should have done it when you first came back after mother died, we get a divorce."

"Do you still talk to him? Mr Mafioso."

"Charlie, I forgot about him, he was gone, could you not see it was you I wanted."

"No thats why you have brought up a divorce again, so you can swan back off to Sicily, to that prick. It's in the DNA isn't it, they say that don't they, that in the Mafia you always marry within it." He started to laugh that mocking arrogant laugh he sometimes had.

"He wants to marry the boss's daughter thats it isn't it."

"I have not spoken to Salvatore since he told me he

was changing his phone number, because I told him I could not just jump on a plane and fly back to Sicily. Thats over four years ago, I have tried so hard to be as you say, 'the dutiful wife,' but I wanted to be your lover too, to share that passion we once had. So, no I am not saying I want a divorce, so as you say I can swan off to Palermo. I am sure after all this time; he has moved on like I have."

"Oh Gigliola"

"Don't you call me that"

Charlie sensed a way to get at her.

"Oh, thats it, Gigliola, did he whisper it in your ear as he fucked you, you slept with him didn't you? Do you miss his dick Gigliola? Mr Bloody Mafioso. Why do you think I don't want sex with you anymore? Your soiled goods, why would I want to touch you, after he has had his bloodied hands on you"

She went to slap him, but he grabbed her arm, so she missed and just hit fresh air. He pushed her on to the floor and went upstairs. That was the first time she had ever seen any kind of violence in him, and it scared her. He was not normally violent. As it turned out he prefered a more sophisticated kind of violence, mental torture. He started to dress in a black suit, complete with black silk shirt. He stopped calling her Janice and started to refer to her as Gigliola, always saying it in a slow seductive tone, then he would laugh. It didn't stop there.

He would ask her to undress him, because he knew how much, she had wanted to do that to the 'Italian' he always called him Italian because he knew it meant a lot to her that this guy was Sicilian, so it was another way of hurting her. He would play along with the undressing, even sometimes got an erection, but that all added to the fun. He would get her all aroused, kiss her neck fondle her breasts, then just as she was going to remove his bikinis. He just switched off, and said he didn't feel like it anymore. This little charade went on for months, she was almost on the point of suicide, she was not sure how much more she could take. She asked, begged for a divorce, but he said no, no she was not going to run back to him, he didn't want her, but he was as sure as hell going to make sure the Italian didn't have her either.

She started to hope that Liggio was her real father, he would sort Charlie out. Then she recalled what he had said about DNA. Maybe he was right, if she wanted to know the truth could she get Liggio to take the test? She realized that wanting him to be her father, in order Charlie be dealt with, that made her no better than him. The thoughts were coming fast and furious. If he was her father, did that mean she was a Mafioso in her own right! Somehow, she found comfort in that, the same kind of security she had felt when she realised 'Yin and Yang' were following her. The Mafia said, 'That revenge is a dish best served cold.' She would have her revenge on Charlie for this mental torture, but she would bide her time. She suddenly felt as if she had gone somehow to a higher plane, found that inner strength, that would enable her to cope with his taunts, his sick charades. She even found a way to turn the tables.

She first did it when he wanted her to undress him, she took of his jacket, kissed his neck, undid his shirt, then she called him Salvatore.

He didn't bite at first, pretending he had not heard her. But she was not done yet. She took his shirt off then slid her hands up and down his chest.

"Oh, Salvatore I have dreamed of this moment, take me Salvatore to your paradise." she whispered in his ear.

"Bitch" he pushed her away

"Oh, Charlie why whatever is the matter. Don't you want to be in my fantasy, not much fun is it, when the shoe is on the other foot. Papa would be proud of me"

Her turning the table had the desired effect, it ruined his enjoyment of taunting her, he stilled called her Gigliola to get a dig at her that way, but she got used to it, and he could never say it like Salvatore had, so she just saw it as an irritation.

It was the 15th of November, a day she was never likely to forget for two reasons, she had stopped listening to the radio because it had started to annoy her, as she worked at her studio. So, she had not heard any news. She was surprised as she turned into the driveway to see Charlie's car. He was not usually home this early. She went in the house took off her coat and scarf and called to him. She heard him reply from upstairs, so went to see if he had taken his shower, he always did that when first coming home, it helped him relax before they ate their evening meal. Although they were technically more like housemates rather than man and wife, they were civil to each other, all that was about to change.

She found him in the bedroom, piling clothes into a suitcase.

"Are you going on a business trip, you never said anything this morning."

The glance he sent in her direction sent a cold shiver down her spine.

"You don't know do you?" he said in that mocking

voice he sometimes used when he was about to belittle her.

"Heard what, it's not the family, something has happened, I haven't had a phone call."

"Well, why would you, so sad daddies dead."

She sat on the bed, what did he mean? She enquired if he was talking about his father, she was unaware he had been unwell, then Charlie did have his secrets, she was sure of that.

"No, not my father, that bastard of yours, he dies in his own bed, something that bastard never gave the poor sod's he murdered the privilege of."

She could hear the anger in his voice, but why should he care?

"Liggio is dead, my father he his dead, my god they got to him, was it poison in his food, he was always concerned about that, but he usually got his cellmate to taste it, just in case."

He gave out a raucous laugh, before going on to say that poison would have been too good for him. While she suddenly realised what he had just told her. The tears began to trickle down her cheeks.

"You're crying for that bastard, my god, you never even knew him, only what you have read and the journalist's account of his miserable existence. Tell me something did you fuck that Mafioso because it made you feel worthy of your murdering father. I have often wondered did it turn you on, that rush of adrenaline, the excitement of fucking a man that killed people."

"He never killed anyone. "She replied with conviction.

"Really, he told you that, what and you believed him Janice, Janice you poor pathetic cow. Well now he is dead, I am done here. You were never recognised as his daughter, so you won't be getting any money. So, I am going from this miserable excuse of a marriage, you can have your divorce. Time to come out of the closet as they say. I am going back to Italy, to be me myself, to accept I am gay, I slept with your brother, did you never wonder why he had no girlfriend. He didn't want me to marry you, but I was hiding from my true self, fucking you was a cross I had to bear."

Her sadness turned to anger how could he be so callous.

"What you're saying, you only stayed with me because of money!! Haven't you enough of your own. But your wrong, there is money sitting in an account in the Banca di Sicilia, in Via Roma in Palermo."

He gave that raucous laugh again.

"Yes of course there is, so why have you never told me about this before, why is it still there."

"Why do you think? It's blood money, taken from innocent people, do you think I could really spend that, knowing where it came from.!!!!"

"You're deluded, so show me the account paperwork."

"No, I won't, haven't you a plane to catch?"

"Yes, your right, I have given you too many years of my life, I should have left you, faced up to my gayness, if I had done that maybe Graham would still be alive now and we could have been happy together." He closed the lid on his suitcase, had one last look around the room. Then made his way downstairs. Leaving Janice sat on the bed, now in total shock. She heard the front door slam, and the sound of tyres on gravel as Charlie turned the car at speed and was gone from her life.

She got from the bed, went to the bathroom and unusually for her took a shower rather than a bath. Her way of cleansing her body of Charlie. Then going downstairs, she poured herself a glass of his expensive single malt and came to a drastic decision. She had another swig from the glass, then went to the dining room, to the writing bureau that had belonged to her late mother. Charlie knew it had the secret drawer, but she had never shown him where it was, because the bank account details were hidden in there. She took out the large brown envelope and went to the fireplace in the living room. Removing the documents, she tore them up ferociously and placed the torn pieces into the fire grate. Then going to the utility room, she returned with the bottle of barbecue fuel poured a generous amount on the papers, and using a large match watched as ignition took place and before long flames, only small but sufficient consumed the content of the grate, she got herself another drink and curled up on the couch and watched the cremation come to its conclusion. She hadn't burnt the bank details, she sat now looking at the amount in the account, 10,000 sterling had been paid in, under her English name, she wondered how much interest it had earnt in nearly 8 years. It was the proceeds of crime, how many thousands of people had died at the hands of drugs, this was drug money, she wanted none of it. So, the bank details went the same way as the other documents she destroyed them. Then sitting quietly, she looked at the painting she had been sent, she had asked Luigi if she could have it back, saying she knew it was impolite to ask for the return of something given as a gift. He was not in the least bit offended was just glad she felt she needed to have it back. She knew it would not be a problem Luigi had always felt uneasy about having it on the wall, because he felt it would not be well received by his customers, giving the impression he supported a criminal organisation.

She got up from the couch a determined woman, no, the painting had to go too. Now was the time to put all this to bed, to move on with her life. So, taking it from the wall she took it outside removed it from the frame then put the canvas in the incinerator and cremated that.

Christmas came and went, it had been strange being in the house alone, she missed Charlie more than she thought she would. They did have some good times, even after she came back from Sicily, how supportive he had been when he helped her cope with the rape. How he had wanted her to report it to the police in Palermo. There had been laughter, silliness, if only they could have got past the Mafioso, she felt sure they could have been happy, from her point of view. Why had he not told her before he was gay, all that pain and anguish could have been avoided. Still, she knew now, and hoped he would find inner peace, and someone he could spend the rest of his life with.

Seventeen

AFTER WEEKS MONTHS of dithering she decided, she needed answers, the only way she would stand any chance of getting them, was to go back to Sicily, she decided to go in early May. Because Friday was a bank holiday she booked her flight for Thursday, this time she was not taking the ferry. She had booked a week at the President hotel, so she had a room even though she wanted to go to Cefalu. There was one thing she could do, find out the truth, about how Antonio had died? She knew she had to go to Corleone, Luciano might not have been her father, but Charlie had done a good job manipulating her, while he had still been alive, she had started to believe he was.

They were flying over the island to prepare for landing. She looked out of the window, she felt emotional, then she had felt like that a lot in this last year. How was she going to cope being back in Sicily? She had so much she wanted to do, so she would not have time to think about it too much. She took a taxi to the hotel, and was pleased to see a familiar face, Fabio was still working there but was now restaurant manager. She had asked if she could have the same room as she had used on her original visit. As she walked along the corridor she saw her.

"Maria, Maria," she dropped her suitcase and ran to greet a startled maid.

"Excuse me."

"Signorina Liggio."

"Yes, yes "Maria hugged her, and proudly showed off that she still wore the bracelet she had been given.

The hotel had changed dramatically since her last visit, she was disappointed that there was no longer a bath but now a shower in her room. She did not know why she did it, but she went to the window hoping to see Salvatore there, when she must have known he wouldn't be. It was late afternoon, she unpacked her suitcase, put her bits and pieces in the bathroom. She ordered room service some tea and toast and planned what she was going to do that evening. Tomorrow she would go to Corleone.

She decided to stay in the hotel, it had been a hectic day. Not only that knowing that Salvatore and Leonardo were not out there she felt vulnerable. She had wondered if she should go to Ansa's office to explain herself. But thought as the saying went 'Let sleeping dogs lie.' It might be better to just forget about all that. Although her introducing herself to Maria as Liggio had been a faux pas. It would surely get around the city that she was back. But as she kept telling herself would anyone really care. Any Mafia talk now was about the new boss of the Corleonese, Leoluca Bagarella. If she was hot on the grapevine might Salvatore hear she was in Palermo?

Was there a chance however slight that he might want to see her?

Night passed today and she was excited but a little anxious about going to Corleone, not realizing how momentous this decision would prove to be. The hand of fate was going to play its part. She wanted to see some of the countryside, so decided rather than hire a taxi for the day, she would get the bus, if it was like the buses at home, it would meander along rural roads and not as the English said 'Go as the crow flies. It also meant if she decided to stay over for the night, she had not wasted money. Not that, money was an issue. The last time she was in Corleone she was treated like Royalty an American celebrity, everyone, well almost everyone wanting to shake her hand, hug her. There would be none of that this time. But she was glad, she could just mingle in amongst the locals, and for the first time in seven years be herself, although a little part of her now she was back in Sicily, mourned that this was not really her home.

When she arrived in Corleone and stepped from the bus, she wondered if any of those locals that came that day would recognise her now? That scared her a little bit. she remembered how Charlie had bought her red carnations because they were Sicily's national flower, so she would find a flower shop and buy some to Put on Luciano's grave. Maybe Someone sold them outside the cemetery? she decided to buy eight, one for each of the years she had believed he might be her father. It was easy to find the cemetery, it was well sign posted, it was quite busy for a graveyard, then like Luciano a lot of the other Mafia bosses were buried here. Including Michele Navarra. The Times obituary had said Luciano was in an unmarked grave, that his remains had been interned next to his father. she saw two men in what looked like white forensic overalls, she went across and asked them if they knew where Liggio's grave was, they pointed across from where they were standing. She thanked them and followed the names on the plaques until she found it, not far from the grave of Salvatore 'Toto' Riina. Standing in silence for a few moments, she then pushed the carnations in the two small vases mounted on the wall at each side and said she was sorry. The hustle and bustle of other tourists annoyed her. Did they not see this was a place that should be respected.

Above all the din she was sure she had heard her name.

"Gigliola" she felt the hairs on the back of her neck stand up and a sudden chill came over her, Luciano was not talking to her from beyond the grave, was he?

"Gigliola, is it really you?" this time she knew instinctively who it was, there was no mistaking that distinctive tone. At first, she didn't want to turn around in case it was just her wanting it to be him. But slowly she turned on her heels. She stood there transfixed.

"Salvatore "he stood infront of her.

"Hello Gigliola, it has been a long time."

"Wow look at you, the moustache the goatee beard, you look so sophisticated."

"Does that mean I wasn't before" He smiled at her a twinkle so evident in his eyes.

"It's so good to see the face that goes with the seductive voice once again."

"Gigliola this is a sacred place." he said pretending to be shocked.

"Yes, you are of cause right, I was just moaning to

196

myself about all the noise, so many disrespectful people barging around."

"I hoped you would come for your father's funeral."

"The police would probably not have allowed me too, maybe he told the family he did not want me here?

"Tell me, how did you know I was here today?"

"Ah well I did have some help, see that elderly gentleman behind me, thats Giovanni, I paid him to be my watchman, asked him to ring me straight away if he saw a young lady, who seemed to spend a long time looking at Liggio's grave or putting flowers on it. I nearly broke my neck to get here before you went.

She looked to the side and saw down the path outside a hut an elderly man who seemed to be staring at them.

"Gigliola, can I kiss you?

"Do you need to ask?" she had longed for this moment to feel his lips against hers, once again.

" He walked towards her took her in his arms and bent over her, his lips gently pressing against hers, the passion was undeniable. The old man started to shout. Salvatore momentarily, stopped, turned and shouted back.

"Bella Bella" then he turned around and kissed her again he held her so tightly. Almost as if he feared if he let go, she would vanish into thin air, as if she had been nothing more than a mirage. A few people stared at them showing some sign of disgust, but neither of them cared.

"But this is wrong, you could be married." That was her subtle way of finding out if he was.

"No, I could not give love, the love I have for you to another woman. when I said goodbye to you at the airport, when I realized you were leaving me, I felt broken inside. I used to make fun of people who told me they believed in love at first sight. Until it happened to me. Look we have so much to talk about, but not here, not infront of your father's grave, I do not want him to come back and haunt me." he gave another little laugh

Maybe it was the way she looked at him, but it had said more than a thousand words.

"I didn't want to seem presumptuous."

" Oh, Salvatore I just want to show you, your love is reciprocated"

"Let's go then we have the rest of our lives to talk. "He took her hand and kissed it, they left arm in arm, then she stopped.

"I won't be a minute." she dashed back into the cemetery and went up to Giovanni, put both hands on each side of his face and kissed him full on the lips. Salvatore stood just inside the gate, he wondered why she had gone back in

"Eh Giovanni," Salvatore shouted, he went on to say something in Italian. To which the old man shrugged his shoulders. She placed some money in his shirt pocket.

"Thank you, Thank you." she said kissing him again.

She then ran back to Salvatore like a love-struck teenager on her first date.

"I think you have just made an old man very happy. But I am hurt you have only just come back and already you want to kiss other men." he laughed and kissed her again.

My god she could feel herself filling up with sexual tension, she could not wait to make that dream turn into a reality, once more."

They walked a few streets, dodging the numerous tourists who had come to Corleone. Then they arrived at his house. One of those quaint brightly coloured house's Luciano had painted in the picture she had been sent.

"Wow what a beautiful house."

"Thank you, come inside and have some tea." he had said that to make sure she wanted him. Far more than the belief she thought he was a Mafioso.

"Tea, seven years and you think I have come all this way just for a cup of tea. To quote a famous tennis player 'You cannot be serious.'",

"Why, do you want coffee?" he smiled at her knowing now he had his answer. She just wanted him with his clothes off.

The house was just as beautiful inside as it was out. She glanced around the room and saw a painting. She went to look at it.

"Yes, I thought I should have one of his paintings it could be a good investment.

He smiled. He had such a beautiful smile it would make the most miserable of people cheer up just a little bit. She took her shoes off because he had a large white sheepskin rug, in the middle of the floor, she had never seen one so big. It looked pristine so she did not want to stand on it in case her shoes were dirty.

"You like my rug?" he had seen her gazing at it. He wanted her even more now."

"Yes, I am one of those people who are touchy feely, I love the softness of sheepskin on my bare feet, the plushness of velvet, fur."

"Naked skin" he asked seductively as he took his shoes and jacket off.

"Have you forgotten how I caressed your body at Antonio's, come let me touch your skin again, so my fingers can reacquaint themselves with your body?"

"But I am not naked."

"We can soon change that."

"Gigliola, are you flirting with me?"

"Oh no making a statement of intent"

He walked across and stood infront of her, she had never realized before just how tall he really was. She kissed him, really kissed him so he knew without doubt what was about to transpire. She ran her fingers through his jet-black hair, that was soft and silky like the shirt he usually wore. His body odour smelt sweet, like the Carnations she had just put on Luciano's Grave. His shirt was satin, not silk but still black. She let her hands slide up and down his chest. Anticipation building within her. His collar was open, so his neck and the top of his chest were partially exposed. Like they had been that day in the garden. That had been the first time she had felt a physical attraction to him. He had felt the same and that night until the early hours of the morning they had shared the most intimate of feelings. She slowly kissed his neck and nibbled gently on his ears. He groaned quietly as if the passion was trying to escape.

She undid his remaining buttons and took off his shirt, her hands now touching his smooth soft sun-tanned skin, the adrenaline starting to rush to her fingers. She did just as she had done countless times in her dreams, unbuckled his belt opened his trousers and let them fall to his feet. She loved his sky-blue bikinis they clung to his bum like an extra skin. He said nothing just had that look of anticipation in his beautiful eyes. She slipped her dress over her head, to reveal a front opening bra, she had brought one of those just in case, so her breasts sat against his chest before he took it off. His hands fondled them each one in turn, his touch was so gentle she had missed the feel of his hands touching her body. she could feel the sexual tension building to a crescendo, then it all went wrong. He was just going to kiss her breast, when the image of the savage attack by Ahmed suddenly shot into her head, and she pulled away.

"Gigliola?" he could see her physically shaking, tear's starting to trickle down her cheeks.

"Oh, my darling, what is it. If you want me to stop I will. I have waited seven years for this moment, I can wait until you're ready "He brushed the tears from her cheeks and kissed her ever so gently.

She took a deep breath, then as if someone had flicked a switch the passion started to engulf her body.

"Take me Salvatore give your body to me." she begged him, wanting him to know this sudden hiatus had nothing to do with him. She slipped her hands down his back and grasped his bottom. My god what a wonderful bum he had. He pulled his bikinis down. Stepping out of his trousers. Just when it should have been getting steamy, she killed the passion when she suddenly started to laugh.

He tried to make light of it.

"Oh, it's not that bad is it. Has all that time taken its toll. You wound me yet again?"

"I am sorry it's your socks." she said trying so hard to keep a straight face.

"And whats wrong with my socks." he seemed a little hurt that she was laughing at him. That suddenly the sexual chemistry seemed to have evaporated.

"Nothing they are beautiful socks. Like there is nothing wrong with any part of your body either. But please take them off, they are spoiling my enjoyment of the view."

It was then that he realised, it was because the only thing he was wearing was his socks. He saw now why she thought it was so funny. He pulled his socks off, took her hand and slowly pulled her down on to the rug. The soft sheepskin against her skin was a turn on. He lay there just looked at her with his come to bed eyes, telling her he wanted to take her to his paradise, where they would both bathe in the waterfall of passion. They took their time engaging in foreplay, using their lips to caress each other's bodies. Then he used his tongue licking her skin, as it meandered down her breasts, going down toward her legs. It gave her a wonderful tingling sensation. She loved the roughness of his beard against her skin. He had a huge tattoo on his back, it went all the way across both his shoulders, butterfly wings. This was the ultimate way to entwine their bodies, to show their love for each other. He rolled her over, so she lay on her back, then taking her legs he placed them on his shoulders, and slipped inside her, he started with a slow rocking motion, then it got gradually quicker, each time he pushed harder against her, until it was if the flood gate of passion had opened, and he thrust into her so force-fully. at the same time, he was calling her name, in that deep seductive voice she had loved to hear on the phone. Then together they reached their destination, he dropped his head on her chest and tried to catch his breath, she slipped her legs from his shoulders and grabbing his face kissed him. They lay on the rug for some time, just cuddled together their legs entwined so they looked as one.

"Was it as good as the first time. Did I still satisfy you." He asked.

she started to get up from the rug.

"Gigliola?" he took hold of her hand.

She turned and looked at him.

"No, no, oh my god I am such an arsehole." he jumped up and took her in his arms, he kissed her , he wanted to prove that what he had said had come out all wrong.

"Gigliola, my darling Gigliola you took me to paradise, oh my love, I hoped my actions showed you how wonderful it was, forgive me, I am such a fool, I desire you with every bone of my body, I will prove it to you."

He scooped her up in his arms and took her to the bedroom. This time it seemed even more intense, as if the first time had just been a rehearsal, she felt feelings within her she had never ever experienced before, this time she moaned she called his name, she cried, the pleasure, the passion, it covered her like dew on a cobweb on a misty morning.

He thrust even harder within her, his penis making her feel as if it was almost touching every nerve in her body, so they all sang in tune. She wanted it to never end there was such passion, passion she never knew was possible. This time it lasted longer, as if he had deliberately held back the first time, so he could enjoy the pleasure of her body for a greater length of time. Now he was showing her that she did satisfy his needs, she did arouse such intense feelings within him. When it was at an end, he made sure she knew she had taken him to a place he had never dreamed possible.

They lay there giving their hearts chance to slow down. He smiled at her, kissed her again, his lips were soft and sensual.

They started kissing and caressing again, as if they could not get enough of each other, wanted to have all those sensations again for fear they would leave.

"I guess I should start looking for an apartment, should I get one here or in Palermo.?

He suddenly became very quiet, just lay with his head on the pillow. Then he turned and looked at her. This was not going to go well at all. He took a deep breath, got up from the bed, then prepared to drop the bombshell. He turned and looked her straight in the eyes before he answered her question with a question of his own.

"Why would you want to buy an apartment here in Sicily?" the previous gentleness in his voice now diminished.

"Salvatore isn't that obvious so we can be together."

He gave a raucous laugh, reminiscent of the one Charlie had.

"Be together Gigliola, what gave you that idea?" He turned away to avoid any further eye contact and started to get dressed.

"It was good to see you, the sex was as good as it ever was. But it was just sex."

She got from the bed in a calm collected manner, walked casually across to the chest of drawers, then gently picking up a vase, she hurled it towards him, he anticipated she would display some form of anger and dodged it, it hit the wall and smashed shards of pottery lay strewn across the floor.

" Really Gigliola, wouldn't another slap have been more effective."

"Don Aglieri is right, the Corleonese are all peasants."

"You, count your father in that group after all he was born and bred here in Corleone." He retorted in a rather menacing tone.

"Bastard, leave my father out of this."

"Me the bastard, oh no Gigliola both my parents were married, to each other I might add, if there is anyone here with that title, it is surely you. Yes, I am a Mafioso, so now you know, but I never worked for your father, my boss back then was Toto Riina, he ordered your rape. He couldn't be sure you weren't Liggio's daughter, so he edged his bets. It was important Liggio kept his mouth shut. There was a price on his head to start with, your rape was another warning to him."

"Your lying, I need to go, I can't stay and listen to any more of your lies. They got to you, didn't they? If it had just been sex you would never have telephoned me once I went to the UK, you wouldn't have given a shit"

"Think what you like Gigliola, but your right you should go home, there is nothing here for you, now your father is dead. I must compliment you, you were then, still are one hell of a lover. But as they say you can have too much of a good thing. Oh god don't start with the tears."

"Well, how should I feel, I thought you cared about me, all the charm, the tenderness, it was; Your sick, then what should I expect."

"I am sorry, I am just not ready for a long-term relationship, in my profession you learn to become devoid of feelings, of empathy, I thought when I met you, I could change, but it's obvious to me now I can't. Look I must go, take your time, there is tea in the cupboard, just make sure the door is locked when you leave. If it was not for the Mafia maybe we could have had a future together. Look I would like you to have this." He had a crucifix around his neck, he took it off and put it into her hand, gave her a kiss on the cheek, and went, to do whatever it was he had to do.

She went to the sheep skin to retrieve her clothes, but found herself laying back down on the rug, she closed her eyes and fantasised that he was back there naked next to her. Then the realisation that he had never cared that much about her. Still naked she went to the kitchen

With the intention of making some tea, but there was a sudden shift in her mood and anger took over from the feelings of desire. She took a knife from the stand next to the cooker, went into the living room, to her father's painting. Then she slashed at it with the knife leaving it in tatters. Laughing like some demented hyena, his precious investment was now worthless. She was not content with just destroying that, oh no like so many stereotypical wronged women, she found a pair of scissors went to the bedroom and started on his clothes. Finding what looked like his most expensive suit, she proceeded to cut it up, then she did the same with at least four or five of his shirts. Using her lipstick, she wrote her name on his full-length mirror, and the word Ciao in capital letters. Using the scissors she carved a notch in the beautiful ornate bedhead; to symbolise she had just been another notch on his bed post.

She dressed and then calmly made herself a cup of tea, before she left, leaving the crucifix on the neck of a wine bottle on the kitchen table. In a final act of defiance, she left the front door open. She ordered a taxi to take her back to Palermo, where she booked out of the hotel, went to the airport and vowed never to return to Sicily again. Once back in the United Kingdom she reverted to the name she had always known before her mother's death, and got on with her life, her only regret in all this, that she still didn't know the truth.

Epilogue

(In the first person)

FAST FORWARD TO 2020, there was a worldwide pandemic, a virus called covid was sweeping from country to country. The United kingdom's government ordered a national lockdown, had it not been for that this book and the true story it represents would never have seen the light of day.

In the millennium year, I became the voluntary keeper of ravens, at the late Queen Elizabeth the seconds castle at Knaresborough in North Yorkshire, originally as a community project for the 2000 celebrations, a Northern version of the Ravens at the Tower of London. But due to the pandemic, the ravens and I were grounded because of the lockdown.

This meant most of my time being spent indoors, with no writing idea's I spent a lot of time watching the television. I had noticed a trailer for an Italian series set in Sicily about a grumpy police inspector. Let me stress at this point I was totally oblivious to any connection I had with this island. I liked the look of the trailer so decided to watch the next episode. I enjoyed it so much; I was binge watching other episodes that were available on the BBC I player service. I must have watched about four episodes when I woke up one morning with this name in my head Salvatore, I was perplexed I did not know anyone by that name. So, I thought no more about it. But then a few days later I suddenly realised that the character Fazio reminded me of someone I was sure I had met. I don't know why I did it, but I printed off an image of the character and coloured his shirt in black. I know a bizarre thing to do. But it was if my brain was trying to tell me something.

A couple of weeks later I was watching an episode when Montalbano was talking to his housekeeper Adelina. Next thing I knew I had gone to my laptop and started to type, it was as if I had been taken over by some supernatural force, is the only way I can describe it. The laptop became I suppose you could say an AI therapist, by the time my ex-partner who still shared a house with me, came up with a cup of tea, I had poured out my soul to the laptop. I was sat staring into space. I had used the read aloud function on my laptop to listen to what it was I had typed and was now in a state of shock.

I remember George asking me what was wrong, I just replied Mafia. He pulled me from the chair and hugged me at which point I just broke down. I had remembered why the name Adelina meant something to me, it was at the house she owned in Palermo in 1986 where I was raped. That was the catalyst for the rest to follow. I had never dealt with the rape, after I told George about it, well I had too he saw the state of my body, so there was little choice. But after that I just buried it away in the deep recess of my mind, along with all the other baggage. I had penned a children's book, set in Knaresborough, became known as Igraine Hustwitt Skelton, and over the coming years a respected expert on ravens. The last thing I ever thought would be that some fictional programme on the TV would be the key, to unlock apart of my past I never wanted to recall. The fallout from this loss of amnesia would rip my world apart. As you will see as you read on.

I realised the reason I had coloured Fazio's shirt black, with his shades on, this character along with the name Salvatore led to one conclusion the Mafioso I had originally known as one half of 'Ying and Yang.' My mafiosi bodyguards. After Salvatore had crushed me back in 1994 when he revealed he had never really cared that much about me, I had dealt with it all by pretending it never happened. But now it was all back out in the open, all those questions I wanted to be answered that never were, could they possibly be answered now. If I wanted to step back into my past.

I had previously had a book called 'The comical Exploits' of Gabriel raven 'published and had been working on a book about the supernatural occurrences of the bible. But was suffering from writer's block. I had been talking to my editor about this ongoing problem and mentioned that I had been a party to sudden recall about a part of my life, I had wanted to forget. As soon as I mentioned the word mafia, she was intrigued it would make a great book. It might help lead me down a path that would provide the answers and finally give me the closure I needed. I said there was not enough to fill a full-length book. Unless I wrote it as creative non-fiction. I was surprised she had not heard of that term. So, I had to explain it would be a mixture of the facts of my situation, along with fiction that blended into the truth to give a cohesive story. As you can see, I decided to write the book, how I wish I hadn't. My world was going to come crashing down. Not because of the Mafia, but my very own daughter.

She was my go-to person, I valued her opinion she is very forthright and would not mince her words, so I gave her a copy of the manuscript to read. There were a few things she felt came across as a little old fashioned, but overall, she felt it was a good story. She asked if the character Charlie was supposed to be based on her father? I said he was just a fictious character to marry the fiction to the fact. It was when I started to talk more about Salvatore that she started to worry. Something I was not aware of, until her father said she had expressed her concerns to him, that I believed that what I had written was true, a reality. She started making little digs at me, at a family dinner at a local steakhouse, she asked if Salvatore liked steak. Her husband chastised her in a friendly way. I just replied I wouldn't know we had never eaten together.

We were now in 2021, the manuscript had been sent to my publisher and it was good to go, originally I had titled it ' My Mother's lie' it would be published in the genre of fiction, I had asked for this, and had made the ending the fictional part of it, so it looked as if it was not really true. I had written it like this to protect myself, there were things that happened in 86, that I still feel unable to talk about. That could cause me serious problems with not only the Mafia of today in Sicily, but with the police authorities, and the anti-mafia commission. It is as the saying goes, 'an itch I need to scratch' but not at this moment in time.

I had originally planned to go to Sicily in the spring of the following year, when hopefully the pandemic would have abated. But a sudden windfall meant I decided to go in December. I joined Facebook to promote the ravens back in 2014, so I decided to also have my own profile under my Sicilian birth name. I spoke no Italian or Sicilian, so decided it might be prudent to make some friends in both Palermo and Corleone, just in case I found myself in a precarious situation. That way I would have someone who could speak on my behalf should the need arise. The first few people I sent friend requests too, accepted me, I thought it only right to be upfront and honest, so I told my new friends about Liggio, bad move they all except two unfriended me. The two that were more liberal, both funnily enough were called Salvatore. A very popular name along with Giovanni it seems. One was just getting over the breakup of a long-term relationship, he had a young daughter, we became good friends so that when I went to Palermo I took a large case jampacked with Christmas presents for his daughter, it would be the first Christmas she would not be spending with both her parents. My daughter was furious, what about my grandchildren, should I not be spending money on them, not some child I had never met and even lived in another country. This caused a huge fallout, and my daughter said she would no longer visit, and I was not welcome at her house either. This was just the start of the slippery slope.

I think at this point I should address the issue of my children, in the preceding pages Janice/ Gigliola was childless. I have as well as my daughter an elder son. When I first went to Palermo, they were only two and three. They are now married with children, I wanted to protect them from the media attention that the book might attract, so when I wrote the book. I left them out of the account of my Sicilian encounter I wonder now, if I had never suffered from this amnesia, would I have sat them down and told them about it? Well, they know now, so they have to live with it. Maybe one day we will be reconciled, but my daughter has told her father I should move to Sicily, so sadly that looks highly unlikely.

I was beginning to think my trip was fated, I had my lateral flow test. Flights accommodation booked; coach booked to get me to the airport. But fate and destiny did not want to make my life easy. I booked in, luggage off to the plane, into the departure lounge, then sitting in the boarding area, called to board the plane. Got to the gate, gave the attendant my lateral flow test, then the slap in the face. My test had expired four hours before we were due to take off. So, I could not get on the flight. There was another lady going home to Palermo, who was also denied the right to fly, we had to sit around until we could be taken out to the front of the terminal by the back door, so to speak. I was devastated, so close, but so far away. Was fate destiny trying to tell me going back to Sicily would be a bad idea. I was advised to get another test done, sadly I could not have it done at the airport because the flight was due to leave, so I was booked on the next available flight which was Friday the 10th, so that was that. I rang George, he thought I had arrived in Palermo and was shocked when I said I was still at Luton Airport and would be coming home. I then rang Salvatore, who didn't speak English, I tried to explain the situation, he nodded as if he understood, and I rang off.

As it turned out this delay had been a god send, because when I got home my books had arrived from the publisher, so it meant I would now be able to take some copies with me to use as a conversation starter, the only downside it was currently only in English not Italian.

I had another Facebook friend who lived in Corleone, we had become very close, and it looked highly likely that we would become lovers. Which was as it turned out became so. Not only that I was falling in love with this man. He was a shepherd, who it seemed prefered the company of his sheep. But I knew I had to derail the love train, after all we lived in different countries, not only that; had I not only come to Sicily to seek answers about my presumed father to find out if it was true or had all been the rantings of a drugged-up woman. But then all that evidence, the journalist's believed in it being true. I felt I was in a catch twenty-two situation.

Things became difficult between Luca and I; he was sure I was lovers with Salvatore, that I would not be loyal to him. Not only that, but he felt I was just making fun of him, that I was trying to belittle and humiliate him for a laugh. He did point out once, that he could be someone's best friend, or their worst enemy. I would find out in the coming months just how true that would turn out to be.

My trip was eventful, for all the wrong reasons, I had problems with my apartment, the electric kept tripping, once when I was in the middle of a shower. I tried to telephone but could not connect, so I had to telephone the UK to get George to ring my daughter, so she could email the owners. What a palaver, it happened again, only this time I knew where the fuse box was, and thus able to reset it myself. I was going to have a baptism of fire.

Once back in the UK I did a review on the booking. com website. I was honest gave the positive parts of my stay. In fact, I enthused about the fact I had the whole place to myself, there were two other rooms, but except for one night, there were no other guests.

It was Christmas morning, Luca had video called me, to wish me happy Christmas. Which I thought was a lovely thought. But the euphoria of that would be torpedoed by an angry phone call to George by my daughter. She had received an email from the proprietors of the guesthouse, who were less than happy with my review. To undermine me, they had told my daughter; 'I might be a Mafioso the daughter of that murdering bastard Liggio, but there was no way they were going to pay me any protection money'. Well as you can imagine my daughter was already not happy with me, even less so now. I got a mobile message from their daughter who spoke English and screamed down the phone at me.

I was furious, I had not told any lies, been open and honest, and I most certainly was not a Mafiosa, didn't you have to kill someone to be one of those? Even Luca started to believe it was true, said I had threatened to set fire to the building if the money was not forthcoming. I remember saying to him, it was rubbish they were trying to undermine my book, where they all mad in Corleone.

I then realised, that this meant there were some in the town who believed I was tainted with the mafia brush.

The New year came, George moved out, went to live with our daughter, before he got his own place. Luca unfriended me, I despised that damned book, why had I ever written it. It soon became known to the rest of the family, and everyone turned against me. My aunt who was having an 80th birthday party, said she prefered if I didn't go, concerned about any unwanted guests. I told her there was no danger of any gangsters turning up with orders to shot me. Things were going to get even worse, my daughter decided to message Luca, to tell him to she was worried I might start to stalk him and his new girlfriend, who he would later tell me was in fact his wife of 22 years. His response to my daughter was he sent her a naked photo I had sent to him at his bequest, well that was it. Next thing I knew two paramedics were at the door, saying they had been called because there was a woman at the property in some distress.

I was bemused, by their arrival, they were adamant I needed to go to the hospital, it turned out my daughter who worked for the NHS had called them, she had obviously decided that it was not a sane thing to do, send nude photos to other men. (One and he was my lover and had sent them of himself to me. I might add!!!!!)

George told me she believed that everything in the book was a figment of my imagination, and I needed serious help, the only way I would get that, was if I was sectioned under the mental health act. Who would believe that sudden recall would result in the fallout I was about to find myself engulfed in. The next day after the visit from the paramedic's a psychiatrist and a gentleman who was training to be a GP, turned up at the door. I invited them in, the senior doctor was patronising, but I let it go, I explained why my daughter was concerned, showing them a copy of the book, because as I have touched on previously, there were reasons why I had to be diplomatic with the truth, but I was confident I had been able to highlight the fiction of the book, from the fact. Not so it would seem because over the next month I had several visits from various medical professionals and even the police (which did worry me alittle bit.) But turned out they had come because I had gone to my daughter's house, and she had called them when she saw me at the backdoor of her house on her doorbell camera.

I was so frustrated, I talked a lot about the rape, it was good to finally come to terms with that. All the time these people were trying to trip me up, but I knew I was not mentally challenged that I had been to Sicily that I had been raped, I knew I was telling the truth, yes, some parts of the book were fiction, but the rest was the truth. Things came to a head when I was told a senior psychiatrist wanted to come and see me. I needed George to stand in my corner, he knew it was true, but my daughter was a head of me, she asked her father to lie, because she said I really was mentally unstable, that going to Sicily and sleeping with another man, was not normal. When I knew she wanted my only witness to lie, I really did become distraught. I went to see George pleaded with him, that this was my life we were talking about. Would he let our daughter lock me away with people who really did not know what day it was, or maybe even didn't know who they were? Much to my relief he said he had already told her she was out of order, that it was the wrong thing to do. Yes, he agreed my behaviour was open to question, but I could do what I wanted with my own life, and she would just have to come to terms with my Mafia past, and at the end of the day I was her mother.

I knew the nightmare was over, when the police came again, they had been sent by their superior to ask if I wanted them to investigate the rape. I was shocked by this sudden turn of events, at last the end of the dark tunnel had been reached and I walked out into the dawn of a new day, my sanity no longer called into question. But so many questions still to be answered.

I decided to return to Corleone in May of 2022, much to my daughter's disgust, George had said he would come and stay at my house so he could look after the ravens and the other birds I had.

For reasons only known to him, Luca Oliveri the shepherd had unblocked me, although we were not messaging each other. I had unfinished business with this man, he had gone against my wishes, the Sunday night before I was due to fly home. I had let it go because I thought we had something, now that was proved to be no longer the case I wanted him to be held accountable for his act of sodomy against me.

My problem was other than Luca's name I had no idea where the police would find him. But I am a creative person, and came up with a solution, I was working on a new book about us, using our Facebook messages to tell the story. So, I designed a flyer that gave details of the forthcoming book, in Italian with Luca's picture on the front. I would then display them around Corleone.

It worked rather better than I thought, I had only been in Corleone a day and had only just started to display then on lampposts railing anything I could fasten them too. Luca spent Sunday afternoon going around town ripping them down. He caught up with me at the waterfall on the outskirts of town a local tourist attraction. As soon as he saw me, he came charging towards me like a greyhound just released from the gate. He snatched my bag ripping the strap, looked inside it then shoved it back, I was perplexed there were still several flyers in there why had he not removed them? His wife came towards me smirking, I screamed at her did he stick his cock up her arse as well? Seeing red I pushed her, she fell backwards and bounced off a bush. Luca told his two male friends they should call the police. I screamed 'that was a good idea; yes, I was a mafiosa my father was Liggio, and he had just assaulted me. I was physically shaking, wanted to burst into tears, but was not going to give him that satisfaction. Once I calmed down and the police arrived, I smiled to myself. My father would have been proud of me, it had worked far better than I could ever have expected. The police took me to the carabineri barracks, Luca and his entourage followed in his car. We were interviewed separately, he would have had to give them his details full name and more importantly his home address. That was my way in. Now he was known to the police I could tell them about the sexual assault at the hotel last December. I gave a separate statement relating to that, it went before a judge, and as sexual assault is considered a crime in Italy the judges accepted my version of events, I was advised to get a lawyer in Palermo but was free to go back to the UK.

Once home George asked if he could move back in with me, he was unhappy in the sheltered housing and it was costing him a fortune in rent and council tax, having no one to split it with, so, I agreed. Things were going to go downhill, with regards my trip to Sicily. Word had got around Corleone that Liggio's daughter was throwing her weight around and causing trouble for Luca Oliveri. I started to get menacing messages from a Mafioso called Anthony TR, he said I had to stop going around saying I was Leggio's daughter, that Luca Oliveri was a good guy, who had sadly made a tragic mistake by having anything to do with me. This guy even started to bother my daughter, suddenly I was swamped by trolls, Oliveri had decided to be vindictive and had shared an image of my breasts over social media, he had put a tagline, The Naked Mafiosa, so called, because she spends more time with her clothes off than with them on. This resulted with men from not only Sicily but mainland Italy messaging me with the vilest of suggestions you could ever imagine. Oliveri was convinced as was the Mafioso Anthony TR, that My daughter was me under a fake profile, so they were sending nasty threatening messages, in the end my daughter sent a photo of herself with that day's newspaper; to prove she was a real person. Young men were video calling me, masturbating. It was really starting to get to me, George couldn't understand why I didn't just block them. There was only one thing to do, to embrace my Mafia past and put the fear of God into them. Even Oliveri's family got in on the abuse, his brother who had been in prison messaged to give me grief as did his cousin. I downloaded everything and sent it too my lawyer in Palermo. I felt this was intimidation they were trying to get me to drop the court case. But as I was told once it became official, I could not retract my allegation. So, they were all wasting their time. Even Luca started to message, with some sob story, he had his wife and three children, had I not shamed him enough. I was furious, he made out he was single lived alone, if he was having problems at home that was his problem for not keeping it in his trousers.

As for the court case, after nearly two years, the public prosecutor said there was insufficient evidence to proceed, so the case was archived. But I got my revenge, my book 'sex and a Sicilian Sheperd was well received in Italy, having been published in Italian there first. Luca never believed there was a book, said I had just said that to scare him. I was going to give his lawyer a copy, he has since said I should send it to the Antico Bar opposite the town hall in Corleone. I might just do that.

I go to Corleone every year now, I am well received in the town by those who remain loyal to the Mafia, against strong anti-mafia feeling. I have been embraced by Giovanni Riina, who has become a close friend. Last year I was even stopped in the street, by a lady who it turned out was the daughter of Liggio's brother. I could have got my answer if she would have been willing to do a DNA test, but I have decided I should leave well alone. I hope this explanation has helped clarify the truth for you, as for the secret I keep hidden from view, I have already thought about this and have a title 'The Mafia's Pizzeria Puppet'. Will I write it, now I honestly don't know. I am currently working on the sequel to the book about the shepherd, which follows on from the point in which he unblocked me again.

The End

Luciano Liggio

My presumed father was one of ten siblings, born into extreme poverty, in the mountain town of Corleone in the region of Palermo. He first turned to crime in his teens, stealing grain to help feed the family. He was arrested and sent to prison for six months. On his release he took revenge on the man who had reported him, by shooting said man dead.

At twenty he came to the attention of the Mafia Don of Corleone, Michele Navara who hired him. In the late forties while in prison again he formed a friendship with Salvatore Riina, Bernando Provenzano and Calogero Bagarella, all natives of Corleone, once they left prison they formed their own gang.

Liggio kidnapped murdered and then threw the dead body of the trade unionist Placido Rizzotto into a ravine. He had been causing employment issues for the wealthy landowners, and Navara so he had to be stopped. There was now a new thorn in Navara's side Liggio himself, who was getting illusions of grandeur. Liggio decided he wanted to be the boss, and this concerned Navara, there was only one solution, have him killed. But the attempted assassination left Liggio with nothing more than superficial injuries. This attempt on his life, angered him he was well known for being a hot head, one Mafioso was reported as saying, when you were around Liggio you had to watch how you looked or spoke to him, if he felt anyone appeared to be showing disrespect, he took out his gun and shot them. So, it was no surprise that Liggio had Navara ambushed as he drove along a country road on his way back to Corleone, his car was riddled with bullets, he along with an innocent doctor he was giving a lift to, had no chance of survival. That was it Liggio not only took the top prize of head of the Corleonese mafia family but went on to defeat the bigger Mafia families of Palermo and become the Capo di Capi, the boss of Bosses.

By 1971 he started a new sideline that along with the southern Italian mafia clan the 'Ndrangheta of kidnapping wealthy industrialists for extortion money. In 1974 Liggio was finally captured in Milan, where he had lived undercover as a wine merchant. He was found guilty of the murder in 1958 of Michele Navara and sentenced to life in prison, but he continued to be in charge, until his lieutenant Salvatore Riina decided he had, had enough of Liggio's laid back attitude, and that a more proactive stance was needed against the state, so Liggio was sidelined, and so began the terror of Riina, who waged war on anyone who stood in his way. He ordered the murder of women children, police, Judges anyone he saw as the enemy of the organisation. He became known as the Beast the most blood thirsty Mafia Godfather of all time. Ordering his hitman Giovanni Brusca to kill just under two hundred people. At the Mafia maxi trials in 1986, Liggio was acquitted of ordering four murders from his prison cell but remained in prison. He had been threatened by Riina not to disclose any information on the Mafia, or he would face death. It is believed Riina ordered my rape as another warning to Liggio, as it was said by the journalists, I spoke to that Riina considered I could be Liggio's daughter, because he himself had not refuted my claim, when the journalists had spoken to him, and seemed willing to meet me, maybe for reasons none other than curiosity.

Liggio died in his cell in the high security prison in Sardinia in November 1993 of a heart attack. his body was taken to the cemetery in Corleone, where his remains were put in his late father's tomb, but his name is not included.